Currents 2020

Editor's Note

Dear Reader,

    As we all know now, times change rapidly. The spring semester of 2020 displayed this effectively as Covid-19 disrupted our lives. But time and time again I was surprised by everyone's resilience. Despite the heartbreak of leaving, the uncertainty of the future, and the sadness of the present, we forged forward. Of course, I should have known that weathering storms is no trouble for Captains of our caliber.

    Thus I present to you *Currents 2020*. First, I'd like to thank everyone involved in this edition's creation. To my staff, your work was absolutely invaluable and I wish you the best going forward. To Dr. Rodden, thank you for your continuous support this year. I'd also like to thank the staff of last year's edition, who kindly guided me through many unforeseen difficulties. And, of course, thank you to all who submitted.

    Secondly, I'd like to announce the theme. This year *Currents* did not pick a theme in order to encourage submission of all types of works. After receiving submissions, we then divined a theme from the accepted works. Based on the works in this edition our theme this year is memory. Many of the works showcased in this magazine ruminate on what memory is and the consequences of losing it.

    As always *Currents* strives to showcase CNU students' exemplary talent. I believe this edition follows tradition.

Thank you for reading,

Rachel Applebach
2020 Managing Editor

Currents 2020 Staff

Managing Editor	Rachel Applebach
Assistant Editor	Grace Vivirito
Prose Editor	Andrew Cooper-Stone
Poetry Editor	Heather Holmes
Public Relations Chair	Abigail Barna
Business Manager	Liam McLaurin
Online Editor	Douglas Barger
Faculty Advisor	Dr. Ivan Rodden

Cover painting" River Side,"
oil on composite board by
Grace Brantes-Wherry

Table of Contents

Love Ballad

Colin Jones

Ballads of love are overused
Why not a tale of ire?
The flowers, sunshine, rainbow dreams
No circumstance is dire.

All of them seem to be the same
Cliched beyond belief.
Shakespeare really was not all that
I'll offer some relief.

I've found that love is dead to me
No, wait, that's kind of dark...
Maybe a poem about disease?
Or several angry sharks?

I get why they default to love
It's logical, for sure
Love is a much better topic
Than pestilence or war

Remembering Pete

Jordan Beamer

Pete watched the nurse in the periwinkle scrubs place fresh, folded towels in the bottom drawer of the oak wardrobe next to the bathroom door. He was lying flat on his back with his head turned to the side, and instead of napping, as most Sunny Side residents did in the afternoon, Pete allowed his mind to drift and wander through whatever memories surfaced.

Glancing at the clock, which read 3:19, Pete realized if he did not get up, he would miss the afternoon activities. On Tuesdays, Beta Club members from local high schools visited the residents, and Pete did not want to miss a chess match or the pies. He tried to push himself into a sitting position but felt a sharp pain in his left arm. To his surprise, Pete found his arm was encased in a pink sling, which dug into his neck once he became aware of it.

Pete did not remember hurting his arm and reached with his free hand to remove the sling. The nurse saw Pete, and crossed the room, pushing his free arm down with two gentle fingers.

"Mr. Johnston, you need to leave that on until your arm heals." The nurse's face was stern, but the wrinkles around her eyes softened her expression to one of concern rather than purely authoritarian. Her lips were painted a deep shade of burgundy, and her hair was pulled back into a low bun, with just a few strands escaping around her forehead. Pete thought the burgundy lips did not coordinate with her scrubs, which were bunched around her midsection. Looking at her face again, Pete decided the nurse would be more attractive if she lost some weight; her face would thin out and her scrubs would not cling to her stomach as much.

"Why don't we get you to the lobby," the nurse said, reaching to-wards Pete's feet to swing him into a position where he could stand with some assistance. Pete allowed his feet to be placed on the floor, and when then nurse held out her arms, he leaned his weight into them.

She shifted him from a sitting position on the bed to half-standing, the majority of his weight resting on her shoulders as he draped himself over her like a drunken friend. The nurse turned her body and began to push his weight off of her shoulders. Pete's body settled into a wheelchair he had not noticed before, arms moving to the armrests without conscious thought, and Pete decided that he must be more familiar with the chair than he remembered.

"I'll take you out now, if you're ready," the nurse said, tugging at the hem of her top.

The nurse pushed him into the common area, where old, mustard couches were arranged in a u-shape around a large TV showing the local news. Pete disliked the news. He was a firm believer that local school projects and missing pets were not newsworthy, and if the TV had nothing better to show, perhaps it should show nothing at all.

His wheelchair was pushed next to where Jeannie Bray was seated, hands clasped and resting in her lap. Jeannie was the beauty queen of the Sunny Side Retirement Horne community.

Her hair, stark white from root to tip, was thick and curly, and sat atop her head like she had picked a cloud out of the sky and put it there. Pete observed her outfit of choice as the periwinkle nurse adjusted his angle to better view the TV; Jeannie wore a salmon- colored pantsuit with shoes that could have been crafted from the same fabric. Two large, gold hoops hung from her ear lobes, the holes in her ears so stretched Pete feared a sneeze would cause the earrings to rip straight through. She had a ring on every finger, all of them gold, and most with a large diamond or other precious gem glimmering against the yellow lighting in the room.

Pete eyed her from the side, but Jeannie paid him no attention. He wore a green and blue checked flannel and brown corduroys, which were a little short, exposing white socks peeking out over brown loafers. Pete felt like a peasant sitting next to a queen, so he decided he would rather wheel himself somewhere else. He moved his arms to reach the wheels, remembering the sling strapping his left arm to his chest when he felt resistance. He locked eyes with his periwinkle nurse, and she crossed the room in three strides to his side.

"Everything alright, Mr. Johnston?"

"Could I go somewhere else?"

"The students will be here soon. Don't you want to see Gary?" At the mention of Gary, Pete remembered afternoons spent playing chess and sharing stories with a young boy who wanted to be grown. The name "Gary" made Pete's chest feel warm, like there was a little flame in the center that was thawing his lungs, ribs and stomach.

Deciding he would wait, Pete asked, "Could we change the channel?"

"I like this program," Jeannie said without turning to face him.

"Ms. Bray was here first, Mr. Johnston, I think we'll let her keep the program on," the nurse said.

"Thank you, Dara," Jeannie said, and Pete put together that Dara was the periwinkle nurse. When they had a moment alone, he would tell Dara to reconsider her shade of lipstick the next time she wore those scrubs.

Now that I know her name, he thought, the suggestion will be more personable.

Dara patted Pete's back and walked towards the dining room to help prepare the pies. Pete looked at Jeannie, who was still engaged in the local news.

"This is interesting to you?"

"Yes," Jeannie said, her voice clipped.

"There's nothing interesting about it."

"It's interesting to me."

Pete decided Jeannie was not worth the effort. If she wanted to watch pointless news, who was he to stop her.

The glass doors at the entrance of Sunny Side Retirement Home slid open, and a group of students walked through, pulling out IDs to check in at the front desk. There were seven total accompanied by the chemistry teacher. Gary was the tallest of the group, at least three inches taller than the next tallest student, and a whole head taller than the teacher. Gary had dark hair that threatened to be shaggy but was kept in place with copious amounts of hair gel, and his cheeks were constantly flushed.

Gary and Pete had become friends over the last several months. Gary talked about his family and classes, and in return, Pete offered stories of his youth and his late wife, Sheri. Despite Gary's genuine interest, Pete was more interested in what the world was like for the youth. He often thought, what I would give to see the world through Gary's eyes.

As Gary hung his visitor lanyard around his neck, Pete straightened up in his wheelchair, eager for the impending game of chess. The group of students dispersed to different comers of the lobby, and Gary spent a moment scanning the room before his eyes landed on Pete, who was waving the boy over with his free arm.

"What happened, Mr. Johnston?" Gary said, poignant to Pete's sling.

Pete laughed, but found he still could not recall the memory of his injury. "When you're my age," he said, "these things just happen."

Gary shook his head smiling, like the two had shared an inside joke, and stepped behind Pete's wheelchair, pushing him to a table in the dining area. After setting him comfortably against the table, Gary opened a wooden cabinet in the corner and removed an old chess- board. Once it was placed on the table, Pete took note of how the white squares had yellowed, and the pieces had chips on the edges.

"I saw you were sitting by Ms. Bray," Gary said breaking Pete's attention from the old board. Gary had a slight grin, and he arranged the pieces with great care, putting the black pieces on Pete's side: Pete found it considerate that Gary would set up his side of the board first; often times, he felt overlooked by the outside world. Was it because his skin no longer had its youthful glow? Did the lines creasing his face make him appear uninviting? Whatever the cause may be, physical or not, Pete knew Gary did not judge him as others did.

"Are you two becoming good pals?" Gary asked.

"I was there against my will." Pete shrugged his right shoulder, emphasizing the arm in the sling, "I couldn't make a getaway on my own."

"Either of you want pie?" a nurse wearing blue scrubs asked the two as they began their game of chess. One of Pete's favorite parts of Beta Club visiting day was the large variety of pies. On normal days, the only option was sweet potato, but on Tuesdays, he could have his pick of apple, blueberry, pumpkin, cherry, key lime or chocolate pecan. Pete felt like a king, requesting a new flavor denied to him the other six days of the week, and watching it brought to his table while he spoke of high school with Gary.

"I think I'll have apple today," Gary said. "What about you, Mr. Johnston?"

Pete thought it over a moment, and then decided, "Pumpkin; It's been a while since I've had a good pumpkin pie."

The nurse smiled and turned to the kitchen. Pete noticed Gary giving him a different look, he was smiling, but his eyes seemed turned downwards, as if they were frowning. Was it a look of sympathy? It was hard for Pete to place, and he could not reason why Gary would pity him.

"The big game is Friday," Gary said, moving another piece on the board. "We're playing Woodside. I'm taking photos for the year- book, so they're letting me sit sideline."

"Sounds exciting," Pete said, eyeing the board for his next potential move. "I haven't been to a basketball game in years."

"Do you like watching them in person?"

Pete nodded, pushing his rook to the left. "I can't stand television. If it isn't newsworthy, why show it?"

"TV is more than just news," Gary said.

Pete grunted as the nurse set down two plates of pies. Pete's was warm, and the whipped cream had begun to melt down the sides, creating a pool of white on the plate. He picked up his fork and took a bite, closing his eyes to try and remember the last time he tasted a pumpkin pie as rich.

"Enjoying it?" The nurse asked. Pete mumbled something in- coherent and took another bite. The nurse smiled, and added,

"Just as good as last week's?" Pete was unsure what the nurse meant by this, and before he could ask her, she turned back to the kitchen.

Gary said nothing and kept his gaze on the board, taking slow bites of his apple pie. Pete decided not to give the nurse's comment any more thought.

"I bet that game will be pretty exciting," he said, bringing Gary's attention back to himself. Pete studied Gary's face, noting the lack of wrinkles and absence of acne most boys his age were plagued with. He pictured Gary walking into the gymnasium with a camera dangling from around his neck.

Gary, who towered above others his age, perhaps taller than half the basketball team, sitting on the sidelines and taking photos of the action. What Pete wouldn't give to trade places. He would stroll into the game, camera swinging left and right, perfectly in time with his confident gait. He would have a camera strap digging into his neck instead of an arm sling, and instead of pumpkin pie, he might buy a hotdog from the snack bar, his youthful metabolism keeping it off of his stomach, which had grown considerably since his residency and Sunny Side began.

A cheerleader from the sidelines might make eye contact with him, and Pete would throw a wink in her direction. Afterwards, she would approach him and ask if he wanted to go to a party at her friend's place, and Pete, being able to run on less than ten hours of sleep, would agree, linking his arm with hers as they strolled out of the gym. He could win prom king, something maybe unheard of for a school newspaper photographer, but Pete thought his charisma could carry him through. What an ultimate irony it would be to have someone else take a photo of the cameraman's victory moment.

"I could take you, if you like," Gary suggested, pulling Pete back to the present moment. "Take me where?"

"To the game. I could sign you out, a nurse would have to drop you off, but I can be your guardian if you'd like to sit sideline with me."

Pete laughed. "I'm old enough to be twice your guardian."

Gary blushed. "I didn't mean it in that way. If you're with me, you'd be allowed out of Sunny Side."

Pete thought it over and realized he had not left in quite some time. "That's allowed?"

"I'm pretty sure. I can go get the paperwork to sign you out on Friday."

Pete's heart raced at the thought of seeing high school again. "I would love that," he said, picturing his grand entrance into the gymnasium. Gary scooted his chair out to find Dara, and Pete looked down to find Gary had won the game while he was daydreaming. His pie had grown cold.

It isn't as good as it was last week, Pete thought. Perhaps the next week, he would order something different.

The following days crawled by, and Pete spent each one in anticipation of his exciting Friday night. His arm had made a steady recovery, and the nurse was allowing him to take it out of the sling, as long as he promised not to exert it too much.

When Friday came, Pete was loaded into a white van, and Dara took her place behind the wheel. Gary promised to meet him outside the school, and as the van pulled in, Pete observed the students hanging around outside, smoking cigarettes and leaning on one another. Gary was stationed at the main entrance, camera in hand. As Dara lowered Pete on the ramp and out of the van, Gary held up his camera and snapped a picture, smiling as he did so.

"I barely had time to smile," Pete protested, but he found him- self smiling too. The exhilaration of being at a high school was more than he could process. He imagined the faces of students inside as Gary wheeled him through the doors; would they stay silent, or would they clap?

"You've got my phone number," Dara said to Gary, who pulled out his phone to check it once more. "Call me if anything goes wrong. If not, I'll be here by 8."

"No worries," Gary said. "I think Mr. Johnston and I are going to have a great night." Pete nodded in agreement, leaning forward in his seat with anticipation.

Dara laughed. "You take care of each other, alright? I'll be back in two hours." With that, she turned back to the van and loaded the ramp inside. Gary stepped behind the wheelchair, pushing Pete towards the double doors.

"You ready?" He asked.

"What I would give to run inside right now," Pete responded. He was bouncing in his seat, and when the door swung open, he was hit with the sound of whistles, cheers and sneakers squeaking on the floor. The sounds assaulted his ears, and Pete jolted back, but Gary seemed not to notice. He wheeled him through the hallway, turning right at the gym, which was packed floor-to-ceiling with people.

"I'm going to park you just behind me," Gary said, "incase a ball gets loose. I can block it for you."

"I'm capable of blocking my own damn ball," Pete said, but Gary chuckled in response. As the front wheels neared the entrance, Pete braced himself. Would he wave as the crowds cheered? He wished he had practiced smiling in the mirror.

The wheels crossed the threshold and Pete readied himself for the attention. As the back wheels crossed too, he realized there was not a single soul in the gym, besides Gary of course, whose attention was directed towards him. As they moved behind the sideline seats, Pete felt disappointed; he had been completely overlooked.

Gary placed him behind his seat and pulled out his camera to take some action shots. "I may have to move around a bit," he said, screwing on a new lens, "but the team will take care of you if it comes to it." Gary snapped a few test photos, then leaned forward in his own seat, eager to track the progression of the game.

Pete looked at the row of folding chairs in front of him and felt more removed from the action than he would have liked. He could not quite make out what was happening on the court. He could hear the sound of the ball slapping the waxed floors and sneakers rubbing their rubber soles, but from his viewpoint, it looked like a sea of bobbing heads moving rhythmically between the two nets. Pete strained his neck to look behind him and saw a row of cheerleaders with glimmering pompoms, eyes glued to the game.

A buzzer sounded, and a player from the opposite team slammed a basketball on the ground in anger. The sound echoed as the athletes retreated to their respective sides. Gary stood up, angling his body to get shots of the players in a huddle. Pete watched him peer through the viewfinder, rotating the long camera lens with the care of a violin player searching for the right pitch. His attention was diverted, and Pete turned once again to the cheerleaders.

One seated in the front row met his gaze, and Pete smiled at her, a genuine smile. Rather than return it, the girl grimaced, and leaned over to the girl on the left, whispering into her ear. The girl on the left laughed, her high ponytail bouncing with the movement, and the other glanced at Pete one last time before looking away completely.

This simple act, the act of being overlooked, was enough to drive Pete to the edge. Using both arms, the left and the slightly weaker than the right, Pete placed his hands on the wheels and backed himself up. He paused, waiting for Gary's protest, and when he was certain the boy was consumed with his photography, Pete continued to back up until he was nearly touching the bleachers. Without a second thought, he turned the chair to the left and exited the gymnasium.

No one questioned the man wheeling himself through the school hallway, and no one paid attention as he pushed through the double doors and entered into the night.

No one noticed, Pete thought. His face flushed as he thought about the cheerleader on the bleachers. How could he have believed any high school students might be interested in his life? Gary was unique, but even his friendship was transactional. Pete knew Gary would not have become his friend without the community service required of him. On Tuesdays, Pete felt like a part of society again, but Wednesday through Monday, he waited in Sunny Side limbo.

There were few cars on the road, so Pete decided to wheel himself further. He rolled past the high school parking lot towards the intersection, where a gas station sat twinkling under the night sky. The scent of gasoline reminded him of fixing up cars in his father's garage, a memory he had not recalled in some time. He began to wonder where he was headed. Pete heard phantom sounds of basketballs and buzzers and remembered. Gary at the gate. As he pushed himself along, Pete hoped Gary was not too worried.

He lost track of how long he was rolling, but his left arm began to ache. The pain was deep, rooted in the bone, and Pete could not figure out why it hurt. He paused to observe it but did not see any bruise that indicated injury. Deciding it was the pain of old age, he continued rolling. At the end of a sidewalk, in front of a foreclosed supermarket, Pete stopped completely.

Rubbing his chin, he struggled to recall why he left in the first place. The game sounded enjoyable, and he wanted to spend more time with Gary outside of Sunny Side.

Pete hoped he was not too far, but he found it difficult to piece together how long he had been wheeling. Before he could decide, a pair of headlights blinded Pete as they pulled into the abandoned parking lot.

The headlights belonged to a van, and out of the driver's seat came a nurse of average height and a stocky build, clothed in black sweatpants and a purple: sweatshirt. Her hair was pulled back into a tight, low bun, and in the glow of the headlights, Pete noticed her burgundy lipstick. He also noticed how her sweatshirt seemed to bunch around her midsection, so he returned his gaze to her face. He decided he would tell the nurse in purple that her lip shade complemented her skin tone, but it was hard to be certain with the headlights shining directly on him.

"Mr. Johnston, you gave me quite the scare," the nurse said.

The nurse stepped behind him, pushing the wheelchair to the van, where she pulled out a ramp.

"After a stunt like this," she said, pushing him up the ramp, "We're going to have to keep a closer eye on you."

Pete felt tired. His arm was throbbing.

"Let's get you back now, I'll let Gary know you're safe." The nurse shut the door and climbed into the driver's seat, and as the van jolted into motion, Pete thought of how to mention the shade of her lipstick.

Pembroke Retirement Home

Andrew Cooper-Stone

I used to sit in a white rocking chair
the hair passing across my face
like spun gold through the sunlight

the wind brushed against my knuckles
kisses of comfort from a previous life
welcoming me in this place

I remember the grass swaying
like laughing dandelions
and I laughed with them, ha ha

I rock back and forth
Smiling lightly at the enjoyment
of a day well spent, rocking away

I can feel the call of my youth
I can't respond anymore
with anything but memories

The Underground Hotel

Jordan Beamer

I shattered a bowl on the kitchen floor when boiling oatmeal leapt off my spoon and stung my wrist. The room had a warm glow from the dying light bulb in the ceiling, and the sun had not risen to shed extra light through the tiny window above the sink. I stood still, scared to im-pale a foot on shards of the bowl.

I heard the click of the hall light, and my father leaned in the doorway. The lighting made his hair look like coarse wool, and a shadow covered his chin like the dark circles under his eyes. He looked down at the broken bowl and spilled oats.

"I keep meaning to change that light," he said, dragging a hand down his face, rubbing the stubble on his chin. This was one of his nervous tics, as if he could wipe exhaustion away with one hand.

My father pulled a flashlight off his belt and flicked it on, illuminating the bowl pieces and warm oats on the floor. The flashlight hung next to his nightstick for no other reason than to say "only an inch separates lights on or lights off," a joke only my mother used to laugh at.

"You're home late," I said, plucking ceramic pieces from the floor. "They pay for overtime."

I grabbed an empty fruit bowl from the counter to scoop the mess into. My father held the light perfectly still, and neither of us exchanged a word until I started picking wasted strawberries.

"Your mother doesn't like strawberries in her oatmeal," he stated.

"I thought she might." Once I was sure there was nothing left on the floor, I set the fruit bowl back and grabbed a new cereal bowl and the jar of oats. The kettle was already half full, and I leaned over to tum the stove on while my dad rummaged through the pantry to find bananas.

"It's two scoops, not three," he corrected me on my hearty third scoop of oats. "Two scoops, one banana."

The kettle whistled and I grabbed it off the stove. My father reached behind me, twisting the stove dial to off while I poured the water.

"Your mother needs her routine." He handed me the banana. "When she does come back, she better not be eating no damn strawberries." I shook my head but smiled as he turned to the living room.

"The bananas get mushy in hot water." I heard the couch creek.

"Take that up to her when you're done," he said, his voice muffled from the distance and a pillow. Within minutes, he was out, but instead of taking breakfast upstairs, I slipped out the back door and took it down to the cellar.

~

The end of lunch bell rang from the hallway, and Tin set his textbook on the desk. Seniors normally ate off campus, but I ate in the library, helping me make an early arrival to class. Students shuffled in and out of the classroom, buzzing on the post-lunch hour high.

"Explain this to me again," he said, propping a foot up on the metal desk tray, rustling abandoned papers in the process.

I ran a hand through my hair, my fingers catching on the knots from lack of grooming. "It's simple," I told him, "I let a backpacker sleep in my cellar, he told a friend, that friend told a friend, and now I've got too many people to manage myself."

"How big is your cellar?"

I shrugged. "Big enough. That's beside the point."

Tin sighed, and his foot twitched, pushing a book with the cover hanging off out of the tray. "I have yet to see the point." "I'm making good money." Tin scoffed, so I added, "If I keep this up for a couple months, I could afford the summer trip to Japan."

"You're sure your dad can't help you?"

"Even with the night shift pay raise, medical bills are stacking. We can barely afford visiting relatives on holidays."

Outside, the warning bell rang, and Tin glanced over at the last few students filing into the classroom. Several of them pushed past him, the majority towering over him with a couple inches. He looked them up and down, and I reached out and touched his shoulder to bring his attention back. "Do you want to help me or not?"

"Run a hotel?" Tin laughed, but it was abrupt, like a cough, and my hand fell back to my side. "I'd rather not."

"Come on, Tiny."

Tin straightened up, as if trying to reject being so short. His arms remained crossed, fitting the angry expression pulling his eyebrows together and turning his mouth downwards.

"I'll cut you some of the profit," I offered.

"I'm not bell hopping for strangers in your cellar."

"You wouldn't be bell hopping," I countered, "though that's not a bad idea."

"My answer is no." Tin sat down, spinning his textbook around on his desk.

"Think of yourself as an assistant manager," I said, moving towards my seat as the final bell rang.

"Out of curiosity," Tin said, flipping open his textbook cover, "how much have you made anyways?" I was one desk over, but the people in between made it difficult to communicate.

Navigating the stream of people, I leaned over and whispered: "Average of two hundred a night."

The textbook hit the ground. A group of three students seated behind us quieted their conversation and looked over as Tin stood and thrust out a hand. I smiled and gave him a firm shake.

"I'm not wearing a uniform," he said, "and I want at least forty percent."

~

The first time a backpacker slept in my cellar, I woke up to a rattling sound outside my bedroom. I slid out of bed, the cold floor jolting me awake. Sneaking down the hallway, hallway, I checked first to ensure my mother was still asleep. I pushed open her bedroom door and saw her full figure bundled in the middle of the bed. The room was full of overlapping shadows, and they hung over my mother's figure as I watched her chest rise and fall in a secret rhythm.

There was no explanation for her decline, a steady slip from fully conscious to a constant state of rest. Over the past few years, fragments of her had come back: moments of conscious conversation with no recollection of time past, requests to see family members estranged from us, and questions about ex boyfriends. Then her eyes would appear to zoom out like camera lenses, and she would be lost to us again. My father and I became caretakers. We put our lives on pause to fuel her recovery. We kept her to a routine she had no awareness of, and if she had moments of clarity, we talked to her until she left us again. Once I knew she was secure, I moved to the back door. Along the way, I grabbed a little league baseball bat from the hall closet, blue with orange flames stretching towards the end, and dust from over a decade of neglect. Outside, armed with a dwarf of a baseball bat and my panda patterned pajama bottoms, I was the definition of threatening.

Bat raised high above my head I saw the silhouette of a man trying to dislodge the cellar lock with a pointed walking stick. The figure turned his head towards me, and I imagined he would run away from the shape of my figure with weapon raised. Instead, he raised his own and charged.

"Stop, wait!" I called out, and he stopped running, but grabbed a log from a stack of firewood, launching it towards me. It arched in the night, and on reflex I swung the bat, feeling the buzz as metal connect- ed to wood.

The log split in half, and we both stood frozen. The intruder could not have been younger than twenty. Leaves and caked dirt clung to the cuffs of his tan pants and his boots, which I recognized as hiker's gear.

The hiker took a step back. "I didn't mean trouble. I thought this place might be abandoned. I was trying to find a place to sleep."

"It's not abandoned. Go, before I call the police."

"I just want a place to sleep for the night, I got mixed up on the trail." It was not the first time lost backpackers had wandered into town from the Appalachian, looking for directions or a place to stay the night.

"I'll pay you," he offered. "I'll mail you cash, name your price."

Perhaps better judgment doesn't exist early in the morning. Perhaps I recalled the trip to Japan, or maybe I felt genuine sympathy. Whatever the cause, something compelled me to set the bat aside, lift the mat for the spare key, and open the door for the gentleman in the night.

~

Minutes before my father had to leave for work, Tin and I sat cross-legged on my floor, separating bills into stacks of 5s, 10s and 20s. Pink fuzz from my over-vacuumed rug clung to our socks, and a breeze would periodically blow through the open window, displacing some of the bills from their piles. The last time we sat in my room together, we made a pros and cons list of our relationship. The cons outweighed the pros, and Tin left my house single.

The cash we earned had piled up after nearly two weeks of visitors; even with Tin's cut, I was making a lot.

"At two dollars a slice, or three-for-five, we should make a profit even if we have two pizzas leftover," I said. Tin checked his watch and exhaled slowly.

"What time is your dad leaving? If he doesn't go before the pizza gets, here, we're in trouble."

I jumped to my feet, stretching.

"I don't understand how you're so calm," Tin continued, putting the money for pizza aside and stacking the rest of the bills in order.

"I've made it this far, haven't I?" I said. I held out a hand and I pulled Tin to his feet. We pocketed some of the cash, placing the rest into the top drawer of my dresser. Tin checked his watch again, and then followed me out into the hallway. My mother's bedroom door was cracked, allowing a sliver of light to trace the hallway carpet. I stopped to poke my head through, and as expected, she slept. I flicked the light off but left the door cracked, though sometimes I wanted to lock it be- hind me. Tin raised his eyebrows, and then took the lead to the stairs. Together we walked into the kitchen, the dollar bills burning secret holes in our pockets.

My father looked through a shelf in the pantry, placing several granola bars in the stained "sack" he carried food in. My father was a firm believer that elementary school children and working women were the only people in need of a lunch box. The proud owner of a "dinner sack," my father carried his food to and from the prison in a bag of unknown origins.

"Get some studying done?" he asked. Tin and I nodded. "I'll see you in the morning," I said as he tied up his sack. "There better not be no damn strawberries," he said, grabbing his keys as he turned to leave. The door shut behind him, and Tin sighed in relief. A moment of peace passed, then we were interrupted by two simultaneous knocks, one on the back door and one on the front.

"You take the guests downstairs," I said, holding the cellar key out to Tin. "I'll get the pizza."

Tin called back for me to tip well, and I opened the front door, handing the pizza man a stack of bills and telling him to keep the change. I wondered how many people had come; the night before had more than expected, but I had yet to run out of beds.

"Beds" referred to the arranged mattresses in my cellar, eight in total. I stepped into the cellar stairwell, grateful for the new light bulb that made all the details clearer. In the last two weeks, the space had transformed. Mattresses were lined up on both sides of the room, and Tin passed out sheet sets to the occupants, who were buzzing about with full backpacks. Two sat on a bed already, rubbing swollen feet pried from dirty hiking boots.

Behind Tin was the water station, one of his early suggestions. We had purchased two large jugs of water and a set of cups. There was currently no running water in the cellar, but Tin was scheming. In the meantime, there was an outhouse a hundred yards away. Tin had also rigged a bell system into my bedroom, so throughout the night, hikers could ring to wake me rather than try and get in the house themselves.

A few of the hikers saw me standing in the doorway and looked up. "I've just ordered a bunch of pizza," I said. "It's two dollars a slice or three for five dollars, if anyone's interested." Every hiker was interested. Tin and I ran paper plates stacked with pizza slices to the cellar, pocketing greasy bills until the hikers had their fill. We sat at the kitchen table in the dim light and split the money between us while eating leftovers.

"I didn't mean to, but I saw your mom," Tin said without taking his gaze off his slice. I swallowed a bite, and the cheese stuck like cement to my throat. I set the rest of my slice down and wiped my hands on my jeans. I trusted Tin not to push for details; he knew I would come to him if anything changed, but nothing had so I never did.

"I'm going to do one last check before you go," I said, noting the late hour on the stove clock.

"Are you sure you don't want me to stay tonight?" Tin said.

"You stayed last night; I've got it tonight."

"If you're sure," he said, already standing to leave. As he walked towards the front door, I handed him his share of bills pocketed from pizza, and he smiled.

"Pleasure doing business with you, Ms. Reech."

I smiled back. "Couldn't do it without you." It was true; Tin was the only person I could trust. As the door shut behind him, I wondered if he felt the same.

Only one bed in the cellar was vacant.

~

After the inaugural guest, I was not expecting recommendations to be made about my cellar, but two nights later I led a new stranger down the stairs, counting money in my hands as he talked. The night sky was black and starless behind us, enveloping us in secrecy like an underground hotel.

"Jackson told me this was cheaper than any hostel," he said. Kicking off his boots, he added, "Convenient location too." A low-hanging light lit the cellar, giving enough light to see the cot positioned to the left that I had made for the previous guest. He collapsed onto the cot and I debated telling him the sheets were unwashed. A wilderness hiker was unlikely to mind, I decided.

"Stops in Southern Virginia are pricey, especially this close to the trail."

"And are there are a lot of backpackers this time of year?" The hiker rubbed his chin, then said, "I would say so. There's a network that keeps in touch." He shrugged. "If you're interested, I can mention your stop on the forums."

The summer trip to Japan floated to the forefront of my mind.

Two hours before the nameless hiker arrived, I was stirring canned soup on the stove as my father packed his sack for work. From an angle, I might have looked like a witch with her brew. I decided there was no better time to ask, so while watching the soup boil, I said, "I want to go to Japan next summer."

My father stood still, which I took as an invitation to continue talking. "The school is taking a cultural learning trip."

"You could learn for free by reading about it," he said. "This would be a great opportunity."

"Maybe you should start smaller."

The air in the room was solemn, and I knew an apology was coming before my father opened his mouth. "I'm sorry things are like this," he said.

"I should have expected that answer," I said, my voice flat like soda left in the sun.

"I'm sorry," my father said again, his voice was sharp like a knife. "We can't afford it." He closed his eyes, as if to remain oblivious to the disappointment that washed over me. Opening his eyes my father glanced at the clock, and then left without another word, leaving me with soup boiling over the top of a pot.

My mind returned to the present, where the hiker was looking up at me from his cot. I thought of the bills in my dresser drawer upstairs.

"Tell whomever you want," I said.

~

Exactly two and a half weeks since the beginning of my underground hotel, Tin and I hit capacity by nine p.m. Eight hikers showed up, and Tin launched himself into making the beds as they trickled in.

Once we had all eight filled, I breathed a sigh of relief.

My relief was short lived when one hiker approached me.

"There are more beds, right? I have five friends trailing behind."

I felt an anvil drop in my chest. "Excuse me for one moment." I crossed the floor to Tin, who was tugging a fitted sheet over a mattress. "There are five more."

"We're out of beds."

"We can't turn them away."

"You want them to sleep on the floor?"

I bit my lip, turning to face the other hikers. "The house," I said, absent-minded as the idea formed in my head. I glanced back at Tin, who looked horrified. "We could let them sleep in the house."

"Terrible idea," he said, "you need to pull back. You've almost got enough money for Japan, anyways."

I shook my head. "It's more than that. If I keep this up, I could go anywhere, or move away after graduation." I went inside to see where the additional five could be housed. Tin followed at my heels.

"Our couch is a pull out," I said to myself, taking note of the living room, "and I could lay out some blankets on the floor to make room for two more. That leaves the fifth." My words trailed off at the sound of the bell tingling from upstairs.

I looked at Tin. "Do you mind taking that?" He rolled his eyes and left as I pulled blankets from the hall closet. I realized the couch had not been unfolded in years, and the springs were tight. Sitting on the floor with my feet braced against the cushion in a wide stance, I wrestled with the handle, ignoring the bell ringing again. I grunted un- der the strain of the couch, and after a pause, the bell rang again. I gave up with a huff and went outside.

In the yard, Tin was surrounded by five new hikers, covered in earth and weighed down with their packs. The sky was a menacing black.

"Your friend is in the cellar room," I said, forgetting introductions. "I can show you to your beds." The hikers tracked mud and leaves through the kitchen. Without asking, they began to drop their packs against the wall, equipment and supplies clattering about. They stripped layers: dirty boots, sweaters, and hats with twigs clinging to them, the pieces piling around the room.

"I was wrestling with the sofa bed when you arrived," I said, giving another firm tug to the handle. One of the hikers covered his mouth with a gloved hand, but could not muffle his laugh, and soon the group was laughing at my expense.

"This is no hostel," one said, "it's a shit show."

Tin stood at my side as I protested, "It is not." I stopped when I noticed where Tin's attention was directed; at the top of the stairwell, a figure in a long gown stood silhouetted.

The figure put a hand on the railing and stepped into the light; it was my mother, looking more alert than I'd seen in a while. She de- scended the stairs, one hand trailing the railing to support her shaking legs. She stopped at the bottom, her gaze moving from me to Tin, then to the five dirty strangers.

"Bree?" my mother said, her eyes locked back on me. "Mother?"

"Mrs. Reech?" Tin added.

"What is going on here? Who are these people?" She surveyed the room, which was a sore sight with dirty clothes strewn about.

"I can explain," I began, but was cut off.

"I have been kept awake for weeks on end with the constant bell ringing, door slamming," she said, putting a hand to her forehead. She leaned her weight onto her heels, her grip on the rail tightening to keep her upright.

"How long have you been up?" I asked.

"Long enough." My mother turned to face the five hikers, who were in the comer of the room trying to piece together the situation.

Her eyes narrowed, and with a hint of strength, she said, "Gather your shit and exit my house."

As the men scrambled about, I noticed Tin trying to slip out the back. My mother noticed too, and ordered, "You stay."

To me she said, "Are there any other guests I should know about?"

I shook my head, but Tin, captured by her fearful spell, nodded and said, "Eight in the cellar."

By that point, the five strangers had left the house in a hurry, and the three of us stood in the living room, looking as though we had been in the eye of a hurricane.

"Have your boyfriend see them out," my mother said with her gaze on me, but a finger pointed towards Tin. Grateful for an excuse to leave, Tin stepped out the backdoor without looking back.

"Tin is not my boyfriend," I said. My mother did not hear my response. Her face looked drained and pale, and I noticed her grip tighten on the railing.

"You'll be paying me and your father back for all the trouble you've caused," she said, but her voice sounded miles away. I could see the focus fading from her eyes. She was unsteady on her feet, and, when I held out my arm, she wrapped both of hers around it.

"Let's get back in bed, mother," I said, putting my free hand on her back to lead her up the stairs. Muttering something about payment, her mind left me again. In her room, I fluffed a pillow behind her head as her eyes shut, and before shutting the door behind me, I set a stack of bills on the dresser.

Anamnesis

Regan Flieg

Crisp, flakey pages
tickle your fingertips as you leaf
through them, scanning
the jumble of narrow, slanted cursive crowded
in the meager margins
in blue ballpoint pen. The pages flutter
like the beating, flapping wings
of doves
or eagles.
They taste like adventure,
like trekking up the towering cliff, sword
in hand and eyes
aimed onward –
the tinge of salty sweat as you lick your lips.
There is the yellow-brown kiss
of a coffee stain on page 83, still cradling
a whiff
of its former fragrance against the dry, musky perfume
of the paper, like an attic
full of old photos and aging trinkets,
the electric pink highlighter fading
but visible,
casting the spotlight of neon ghosts
on sturdy, serif sentences.

Flanders' Mud

Raleigh Hampson

"Let's stop for a minute." Michel set down his basket in the mud and caught his breath. Theoren, his apprentice, waited patiently not twenty yards away, silently and begrudgingly impressed at how far Michel had been able to hike from Zonnebeke before needing air.

Michel heaved but he knew Theoren would want to continue the march to the front as soon as possible, to avoid being seen with him. Without a word, Michel wiped his sweaty hands off on his coarse ala-baster apron, picked up his basket, and started off. Th e horizon before them revealed no city, village, or any sign of human life, only a hellishly desolate pasture of black, trampled mud.

For Michel, the day started off normally: up at five, morning prayers, a feverish spell of bread-baking, and the long hike through a mile of shelled-out earth to deliver said loaves to the trenches.

He often felt, after waking to face a new day of service, blinking in the sunlight through his blasted-in front door, apron on and worn-down breadbasket in hand, the Great War seemed to be a fleeting thought. It mattered little that he scarcely had much dough to knead, or spice to dash, he knew that every crumb past the lips of his comrades on the front lines was a blessing to them, Belgium, and his own soul.

But Michel was not ignorant of the fact that Theoren was ashamed of such an effort, because of the company his apprenticeship forced him to keep. Michel had done him no wrong personally, but Michel's reputation was enough to make the apprentice wary of undertaking any project with him, for the time being.

On this routine morning, Michel could tell that their reluctant acquaintanceship dominated Theoren's thoughts, as his apprentice made a few bold inquiries. Theoren readjusted his grip on his two baskets of warm bread and asked, "If we were to come across one of our own, could he take over for you?" Michel had scarcely opened his mouth when Theoren added, "You're tired."

Michel shook his head and chuckled. Theoren, he rightfully believed, would find any excuse to ensure that the two weren't seen together in public. Irked with his suggestion, Michel replied with just a tinge of acerbic ire, "Never mind that. This is an honorable enterprise; fatigue is no excuse for failing it. All's well for us."

Out of the comer of his eye, Michel saw Theoren curse under his breath at that last sentiment, and immediately felt a pang of regret. Michel wasn't a spiteful man, and Theoren had good reason to want to avoid him.

"All's well for us'," Theoren said through gritted teeth. "Spoken as we walk through a field that was once green and beautiful, towards a terrible world of trenches, misery, and death."

Don't say it, Michel thought.

"Would you say the same if the Germans win this war?"

Michel gripped the wicker handle of his basket until his knuckles were white. But it was a question. Not an accusation. That's more leniency than he was usually granted, Michel's infamously 'antiquated' view—or so claimed of his fellow villagers in Zonnebeke told him—reeked of treachery. But to him, it was simply courtesy. "The Germans are our fellow men, worthy of any decency. How does that equate to sedition?"

"Oh, I'm sure most everybody would be happy to answer that. Try Annette, her two boys were lost in the first months. Or maybe Gines? He's seen what the Germans can do to their 'fellow men,' with their machine guns and their gas."

Michel licked his teeth and said nothing. He couldn't afford to discipline his apprentice and aggravate his apprehension to be with him—without Theoren, Michel would surely have no help in his bread deliveries to the front lines. And Theoren knew it.

"Do these breadbaskets for our soldiers count for nothing?" Michel mumbled.

Theoren didn't reply.

"We'll speak of this later," was all Michel could say, feeling he had to get the last word in.

But there was no time to debate that sentiment. They found a pit not a half mile from the trenches. An eight-foot-deep slough of black mud that appeared deceptively congealed. It was created by the first offensive—this entire plain was the front line not three months ago, Michel recalled. Artillery, squalor, and millions of boot-steps had transmogrified a once-beautiful field into a deathly-quiet mudscape, and this crater was no doubt where an artillery shell was violently laid to rest.

And right in the middle of it, up to his knees, a German soldier cried out for help.

"Bitte! Bitte, hilfen Sie mir!"

Theoren almost laughed. "Speak of the devil. He must be from that war prisoner's march last night."

Michel sat his heavy basket down with a wet *thud* and wrung his hands. He'd heard tales of men and horses drowning in mud, but not once was the desperation of such a thing so clear to him. The mud may as well have been quicksand; air popped and squished with every little movement as the German dared make, lowering him further into the hungry earth.

"Bitte, um Gottes willen!" The soldier's cry rang out with a seldom-heard but primally-recognized dimension of abject terror; Michel's and Theoren's hair stood on end. As the sting of his voice bored into Michel's ears, he started toward the man, but then felt a heavy hand fall violently on his shoulder.

"That's suicide," Theoren growled. "Help him and you could lose more than your life."

Michel stared down at the imperiled soldier. On his dark green uniform there was no ammunition belt, nor holster or harness. The man didn't even have a helmet, his brown hair was stringy and damp from hours' worth of sweat. He was likely a prisoner before becoming trapped and was no threat. Michel said as much to his apprentice.

"Look at him, he's done for," Theoren countered. The mud was already leeching onto the German's knees; Michel knew it would be nearly impossible to retrieve him safely. The German was exhausted from struggling - his shoulders slumped, his upper back slouched, his eyes sunk into their sockets. Emaciated and splattered in black mud, one could be forgiven for thinking him to be a ghoul.

"The two of us—" Michel started, "we can both pull him out." "Impossible."

"We have to try!"

"You are disavowed by the entire village, and yet you'd still try to save this Hun filth?"

The blood rose to Michel's face as he wrung his hands some more. His thoughts and imagination went into overdrive, conjuring images of riots, mob trials, and traitor's executions in the back of his racing mind.

That's suicide, Theoren had said. *Help him and you could lose more than your life.*

Theoren grunted and hoisted up his breadbaskets once again. "They wouldn't appreciate this as a reason for being late."

"Was?! Nein!" The German hollered at them. His voice was cracked and hoarse; it was evident he had likely been shouting all night. "Nein..."

Head hung low, Michel wrapped his aching fingers around his own basket, and started slogging towards Theoren.

Abruptly, an image flashed across his mind: a small tin circle; a medal, lying in the palm of his father's hand.

"From the Congo," he'd said. He sequestered another brass one from the chest of his uniform. "And Mexico."

Young Michel sat at the dinner table as he often did, wide-eyed, as he listened to his father preach of his exploits on the battlefield.

"I ask you, Michel, what man has no mother or father? Or friends and neighbors? Do you think of your enemies as savages? Well, it's hardly savagery," his father had noted, stroking his goatee. "For all creeds and nations, there is abundant glory and honor in war, Michel.

There always has been. I believe it's a good thing. A gentlemanly thing." In all 16 years he lived with him, his father was never wrong. That's just the way it was.

Glory. Honor. A gentlemanly thing.

Michel stopped walking. He looked at his apprentice and wondered for a moment what it might be like to be him, so unbothered by an enemy in need. His wistfulness evaporated quickly. He set his basket down in the mud.

Theoren raised his eyebrows at him. Then his gaze fell, souring into a smirk. "Sir, you can't be serious."

Michel let out a deep breath and stepped gingerly into the pit. Upon seeing this, Theoren refused to contain himself. "I wonder if you had seen what war has become in 1917—the killing, the terror, the gas ...if you might have changed your mind." He turned away. "To hell with you." And Theoren, baskets in each arm, left his master behind. Michel almost thought he noticed a slight spring in his step as he disappeared into the light fog that had fallen over that unholy desolation.

Michel slowly lowered himself further into the pit.

The mud was cold and slick to the touch, yet strangely coarse, like over-flowered dough. Michel knew how to grip such a thing over a table but climbing down a slope of it was another thing entirely. The German, relieved, ceased his cries.

Michel tentatively set down another foot—*squish*. It sunk nearly half an inch into the ground. With great effort, he pulled it back out with a mighty *pop*, falling back onto the slope. His eyes flitted from where he'd placed his foot, to the German sinking in the surface of the crater. Nearly four feet. Too far to anchor himself completely against the slope.

The German reached out his shaking arms. Freezing and exhausted, he likely thought that Michel had given up. But Michel raised a worriless hand. The German understood and nodded. With one hand, Michel burrowed his hand up to the wrist into a slightly sturdier edge of the pit, and wiggled his feet back and forth, allowing the mud to clutch him slightly enough to anchor him, precariously weak though it was.

He took a deep breath, and leaned so far as his frame would allow him. To both his and his quarry's relief, they locked arms without much difficulty as Michel prepared to pull.

In that moment of stillness, he felt his shoes beginning to slide steadily downward. Instinctively, Michel looked around him. Why is the mud thinning, he thought. And then he noticed that he was sweating in the heat.

The sun was rising on a summer day, and it would only be a matter of time before the cold mud became a soupy quagmire beneath its heat.

In a panic Michel locked his arms and pulled on the German's wrists and sleeves with all his might. The soldier began to ever so slightly rise from out of the mud—his belt became visible, and then the bottom of his shirt as Michel's strength waned. The German's face betrayed cautious relief as he gradually became free of his prison in the earth. But Michel's feet began to slide further. The German's sleeves began to tear at the shoulders.

Michel's feet broke through the mud on the slope and stuck out his feet to break his fall, plunging them into the sludge, up to his knees. His heart threatened to beat out of his chest and he began to hyperventilate as the German began to scream madly. The panic lasted for a full twenty seconds before Michel could clear his thoughts. Michel tried to lift his right leg free of the mud, but it only sunk his left leg further down.

He shifted his weight to be more centered, but the chunky mud still clung to his knees.

The shore of the pit was hardly one foot away. If he could find a decent grip, escape was possible. But the German, now up to his waist again, could still be saved.

Do I dare haul him up over me? Michel thought.

Nobody in Vanoverbeke would have blamed him for climbing out of that pit himself and leaving his enemy to his fate.

Except himself.

Taking a breath, he reached over and clutched the German around his waist and heaved the two of them backwards toward safety as forcefully as he could. The mud roared up to meet him, popping and spurting as it reached up to Michel's waist and chest.

He lifted the German over him as far as he could, reaching to the furthest of his ability towards the edge.

Arms burning with the effort, his strength gave out, and the two of them crashed back into the mud, now up to their shoulders. The mud pushed in on Michel's legs, arms, and lungs. He felt light-headed as spots in his vision danced around with macabre vigor.

Exhausted, he could not cry out. The German tried, but his hoarse voice could not muster more than a wheeze.

A few minutes later, a patrol of Belgian soldiers trudged by up above. Curious, they peered into the crater at the two men. They won- dered for a moment if a rescue was worth the effort.

"This man needs help immediately," Michel groaned. "He's a German soldier who—"

And the patrol went on their way.

Prisoners of War

Lacey Beamer

"We were drunk."

It's what they were supposed to say so they didn't say anything important. So they didn't reveal anything. Patrick hoped the words would never have to come out of his own mouth.

"Drunk?" The man squinted at Patrick's face, nostrils flaring as he breathed in deep. Patrick saw the dare in the man's eyes. Squirm and you're dead.

Patrick squared his shoulders and nodded. "Got bored."

The man—Lorenz, Patrick had heard one of the other German soldiers call him—looked to the door behind Patrick, nodding to someone behind the small glass windows set into the wood. Patrick didn't turn around to look, his eyes never leaving the man's face or blood red coat. The door creaked open. The metal legs of the chair that Patrick had seen against the wall when he'd first been ushered into the room scraped along the wood floor as someone dragged it closer.

The chair stopped at the side of the table, and a man sat down heavily. The buttons of his coat hit the metal seat with a clang. He bit into a sandwich and smiled pleasantly. Patrick's stomach ached as the smell of ham filled the small office.

"You Americans," the man said in between bites of sandwich, "only seem to get drunk these days." His heavy accent was worsened by the food in his mouth. He didn't offer his name. Patrick shrugged and flashed the man a toothy smile. "We're in the middle of a war."

"I find it hard to believe every American soldier is drunk every waking moment," Lorenz said, bringing his first down on the table. The man eating the sandwich raised a hand to silence him. He took a bite of his sandwich, chewing slowly. "You're on mission. You must have paid some attention at briefing, no?"

"I'm a gunner," Patrick said. "They tell me to shoot, I shoot." He winked. "Whiskey's good for aim." The second man flung down his sandwich and clapped his hands to shake off the crumbs. He nodded towards the door and muttered something at the first man in German.

The man across from Patrick nodded and stood. He walked around the table and placed a strong hand on Patrick's shoulder. "Come with me," he said, hauling Patrick to his feet before he could move and marching him out of the office into the harsh sunlight. Patrick winced, taking in the fences and watchtowers.

The man marched Patrick towards a long, narrow building across a stretch of dead grass and mud. There was a group of Ameri- cans congregating further down the dead lawn around what appeared to be a food tent. Another group was being put to work digging just beyond the fence, surrounded by guards.

The man yanked Patrick hard onto the steps up to the building's door. The door was heavy and creaked as it opened. Inside, Patrick saw two rows of short beds, most of which were covered in whatever junk the soldiers were allowed to keep. Three men looked up as the door opened, one of which Patrick recognized. It was one of the men from his unit, Chris Healy.

The man still had his hand on Patrick's shoulder. With a final shove, he pushed Patrick inside the building and let go. He left without saying another word. Patrick turned in time to catch the man's sneer.

"What did you tell 'em?" Chris was on Patrick before the door had even shut behind him, finger pressed into his chest. His voice was low so the two men at the other end of the building wouldn't hear.

Patrick shook him off, surveying the narrow room for an empty bed. "That I was drunk. What do you think I told them?"

"You?" Chris doubled over. The laughs echoed in the small room, loud like thunder. A knock hit the door so heavy the entire frame shook, and laughed ceased. "You've never seen the inside of a bar," he said, voice lowered again.

"Orders are orders," Patrick grunted and walked towards an apparently unused bed. He pressed his hand into the mattress before he sat. One of his boots was torn at the toe, and he could see his now muddy socks. He kicked off the boots, letting one of them roll under- neath the next bed. "What did you tell them, then?"

Chris was quiet.

Patrick fell back against the flat pillow, coughing as a small cloud of dust rose from the thin, paper-like fabric. "I want to go home," he said.

"Not a fan of five-star hotels?" Chris waited a beat, but Patrick gave no response. "This is home now," he shrugged. "There are worse ways to spend the war." *Dead* hung in the air, unsaid.

"Home, huh? For how long?" Patrick asked, dispelling the fresh sense of dread.

"I don't know. Until the war's over, I guess."

"Or until they're done with us."

"Come on, Pat. They aren't just gonna let any of us go," Chris said, sitting on the bed to Patrick's right and crossing his feet under- neath him.

Patrick shook his head, raising it so his chin was tucked into his chest and he could level Chris with serious eyes. "There's more than one way to let someone go." He laid his head back onto the pillow, starring up at the ceiling. "I want to go home," he repeated. "And don't call me Pat."

~

Patrick woke up in an unfamiliar bed. He expected the sound of artillery in the distance, or the engines of planes whirring overhead. Instead he heard only the sound of something beeping periodically and a woman's voice cheerfully saying his name.

The woman stood over him, smiling like a bobcat in bright red lipstick. Patrick didn't recognize her. He didn't recognize the bulletin board of photos on the wall behind her, and he certainly didn't recognize the faces in the photographs hung on it. He raised his arm to point and blinked to clear his vision. He didn't recognize the wrinkles and spots on his hand, either.

"Good morning, Mr. Patrick," the woman said, unaware of his confusion. "How are we feeling today? You must've been worn out by all those visitors yesterday."

"Where's Chris?" Patrick asked. If he'd expected anyone to be looming over his bed when he awoke, it was Chris Healy.

The woman reached behind him to adjust his bed. Patrick jumped slightly as the top half tilted upwards so he was sitting up. "I don't know anything named Chris, Mr. Patrick. Your wife will probably be here soon, though. I bet you'll be happy to see her," the woman added, winking suggestively.

"I don't have a wife," Patrick said.

The woman's smile softened at the corners, on the verge of turning down but not quite disappearing. "Sure you do, Mr. Patrick. She'll be here soon, you'll see."

She left the room and Patrick was alone again. He looked around, taking in his surroundings. His bed was the only one in the room. A large window spanned the length of the room on his right, but the blinds were tightly shut. There were more photos in frames propped up on the window's ledge. He recognized his own face in the photos, but not the people with him. There was also a stack of books, but he couldn't see the titles, and a box of checkers beneath them. He didn't recognize any of it. He wasn't sure he wanted to. He couldn't shake the feeling he needed to. He closed his eyes. Maybe, he thought, if he went back to sleep everything would be how he remembered it. He never thought he would yearn for the war, but it was the only thing he was sure of anymore.

"I want to go home," he said into an empty room.

Cannon Fodder

Alexis Ullrich

Hi. I'm Gwen.

I, uh…so, I was a minion for Sundew. You know him. Pretty face, super unimposing, looks like a breeze might knock him over. Y'know. Doesn't look like the type to be a villain, but you all know the shit he did. I did.

I…y'know, I said I was a minion, but I guess the better word would be victim. I was just another victim. I didn't choose that life, and I know most of us didn't. He was one of those kinds of villains who'll force people to do what they want. I was a, a thrall, right? That's the word we're using now? Yeah, that. I didn't want to do any of the things he made me do, but he stuck his fucking fingers in my mind and—I can cuss here, right?

Yeah? Good.

So, I guess I'll start at the beginning, when I was un-fucking-lucky enough to run into Sundew. Like I said before, you wouldn't have thought he was a villain. On TV they always look so obvious, and he was just so damn pretty. Soft face, beautiful eyes that always made him look like he was dreaming. Nicest smile. Real soft hands. He was sweet, I thought. Made me feel nice when I talked, like he was really listening, like I was the only person in the world. Who doesn't wanna feel like that?

I met him at a bar. I was feeling kinda shitty that day for no real reason, and I just wanted to be where people were. Didn't plan on talking to anyone, but there I was sitting at the end of the bar all by myself with some tiny fruity drink or whatever and next thing I know this guy's plopping down next to me and said I looked like I could use company, like a dumb cliché. I guess that should've tipped me off right there. He had this sweet 'n soft voice, too. I thought, why not? Figured I could take him if he tried anything weird. I mean, my mama didn't put me in self-defense classes for no reason. I could take anyone, big or small, and he looked like a toothpick. 'Course, they don't teach you how to defend against getting your mind taken over.

He let me talk, made me feel nice, and eventually I was just going on and on about all kinds of stuff. All the while he kept putting drinks in my hand and they were getting stronger and stronger, just little by little, and I kept talking and talking and drinking and drinking. Didn't notice I was even that drunk 'til I got up to leave and fell right on my face. He helped me up, said he'd take me to get a taxi. He put his hand on my back, and I remember feeling cold. We left the bar. I don't remember what happened after that.

He liked to take people who couldn't fight back, or people who were so sad that they were already vulnerable enough for him to take them over without even having to do much to 'em. Drinks were his favorite tool, and he ended up snatching a lotta people just the same way he did me. A lot of people.

When I came to, I was in some grimy little room that I didn't recognize. I sat up, felt weird. He came into the room, noticed that I was awake, and smiled. Wasn't sweet like before. I got scared. I tried to ask him what the fuck he'd done to me, but it was like my mouth was sewn shut. I couldn't even move my face. He told me to get up, and I did. He told me to turn in a circle, and I did. Told me to get down and kiss his nasty shoes. Guess what I did?

But it wasn't like it was me. I was trapped in my mind, y'know? My body was moving and talking and all, but it wasn't me doing it. It was like I was locked in a cage inside my brain and just watching everything happen. I tried to break out of whatever he'd done to me, but it's not like I have any superpowers or high-tech whatevers. He'd gotten me.

For the next four years, I...

Give me a sec, huh? I don't talk about this all that much.

....

Okay. So. For the next four years, I was his minion. Thrall. Whatever. He took me to his main base and stuck me in with the rest of the thralls—you've seen them all, right? There were a lot of us even back then—and then he forgot about me. Ain't that something? He kidnaps me and mind controls me and then has the gall to go and for- get about me. I was just a grunt now, nameless and faceless like all the others.

You know the game The Sims? Basically, you're playing god and controlling a bunch of people, and there's an option to take away every-one's free will entirely so that when you don't do anything they just do stuff they absolutely need to, like eat and sleep and piss and stuff. That's what it was like being Sundew's minion when he didn't have us doing anything. I hated it, but all that was better than when he actually put us to use.

Most of what we did was terror stuff. You remember that big explosion at the Superbowl two years back? That was us. Me. I remember planting the bombs, and then watching the game and waiting for them to go off. He made us stand there in front of his giant TV, wanted us to. "Watch our handiwork in action." All the while he was grinning away like a maniac. I mean, he was, obviously. Sadistic fucking maniac.

We robbed a bank once, too, when he was still into petty stuff. I, uh…I shot a woman then. I was standing watch over the people that just meant to get their money and be gone, me 'n a few other grunts, while Sundew and his favorite dogs were busy filling their bags with more money than any one person needed, and this woman—god, I still remember her so clearly. She was in this pinstripe dress, looked like she was on her lunch break when this all happened. She had these little pearl earrings, and there was a ring on her finger. Someone's wife, I guess. Had real pretty curly hair, really long, and messy in that way where you know she was trying to make it look like that. She was wearing these dark blue heels, too. I remember those 'cause that's what screwed her up.

She was real close to the door when we put the place on lockdown, that's probably why she thought she could make it out. I mean, we had two guys posted right outside it, but y'know. So, I was staring down one of the tellers to make sure he didn't press the panic button and suddenly I hear this fast *clack clack clack*, and then my body just turned around and fired. The shot scared her so bad she fell flat on the ground. I walked over to her while she was trying to get up and put my foot on her back and my gun to the back of her head. She was begging me not to. Believe me when I say I tried. I really did.

It was the first time I killed someone, I think, but it wasn't the last. That's what we did. Even if we weren't shooting the gun or holding the knife or whatever, we're the ones setting up the traps or planting the bombs or making that poison gas stuff that liquified people's insides. The one and only thing I didn't hate was when we tagged places with graffiti sundews. To him it was marking his territory and challenging anyone to try and take it from him, but to me it was a warning to everyone to be careful when they were out, to not trust strangers. Maybe he'd snatch less people. Maybe one of the heroes would come and find us.

I mean, they did, eventually, but they sure weren't interested in us. Imagine how I felt the day a hero showed up, and then didn't care about us. I forget who it was, some C-list that ended up losing the fight anyway, but still. She was a superhero. I thought she would save us. I forgot that no one cared about us minions, willing or not.

I remember watching her charge into Sundew's base and go on and on about how she was going to stop him—y'know, there's this whole joke about monologuing villains and all, but I've found that it's the heroes who just don't shut the hell up. Anyway, Sundew just laughed at her and ordered us to attack while he sat back and watched. She didn't even try to spare us. I mean, I know I shouldn't be so upset because at that point it counted as self-defense, but still. She didn't even glance at us, just started killing people. She had some sort of enhanced strength, but not enhanced endurance. Sundew just kept throwing people at her until she started to tire out. Then he got up close and stuck her with a tranq. She went out like a light, dropped down among the pile of minions she'd killed or injured. He turned her into another one right after that. Didn't even blink an eye at all the people that had died, either.

I tried not to lose faith then, but then other supers came. Even some more well-known heroes started making appearance, and every time they just squashed us like bugs on their way to

Sundew who always made them a minion or beat them so bad they had to turn tail and run. He never killed supers, he always liked keeping them around. "Add to my collection," he said, and he always kept them as a last line of defense against other heroes. Every new one made me surer and surer that I was never going to get out. They'd kill me before freeing me.

I resented them, too. None of us deserved to die. We were just people who'd been stolen from our lives. Self-defense, whatever. That doesn't mean I'm required to be less upset. I almost died, over and over and over again. And who tried to save me? No one. I was trapped with Sundew in my fucking brain controlling me like a puppet and no one was there to help me, despite all they go on and on about wanting to protect everyone from the dangers of villains. I was everyone. And sure, you could try to say that they couldn't have known that we weren't willing, and I'd agree if I didn't think that was bullshit. I got taken four years ago, and by then we all heard the stories from people like Red Shade's minions when they finally got free of her, and just a year after I was taken was when Delirium was locked up and all his thralls started coming back into society. It's not as if this was some big surprise that villains would force people into doing what they wanted. And, fuck, they all knew eventually that Sundew had snagged other supers, they knew he controlled people, but they still didn't stop to think about us. I deserve to be pissed.

The only thing I'm glad about is that at least Sundew didn't care about us. Sounds odd, but considering the horrible, violating things I've heard other villains do to their minions, I think I'm lucky. Sundew'd pretty much ignore us when he didn't need us to do anything for him. If he did anything extra fucked up, it would only have been to the heroes he snagged. He always kept them around him like trophies.

So. Onto the end, I guess.

I'm sure you've heard the story: Silver Phoenix, one of the greatest superheroes of our time, goes in to stop the dastardly Sundew and end his reign of terror. This is his third time facing Sundew, and this time he finally succeeds, managing to safely dispatch all of the supers Sundew had under his control as well as defeat Sundew. Now Sundew is locked up in Downwater, the highest security prison in the country for super villains of all kinds, and everyone gets to live happily ever after while Silver Phoenix is hailed as the savior of all.

Fuck. That.

Let's start from the top. First, it was Silver Phoenix's third time going up against Sundew. Know why? Because while he mowed through us minor minions, he found that he could not as easily cut down the heroes under Sundew's thrall. They were people, I guess, and we weren't. Did the revelation that Sundew was controlling people make him stop and think about all those non-supers that he just killed? No, not at all. He sure did try his hardest to break his friends out of the mind control, but he didn't even try to, y'know, not kill us. Not even just knock us out, which he ended up doing with them.

Second, and probably the worst thing he did, was letting Sun- dew live. Can you believe that? I mean, I've always hated the idea of let- ting a villain live, especially when they did real crazy shit, but it's even worse now that I know that they probably had no issue killing all of the little people under the villain but suddenly when they've got the villain on the ground and powerless, that's when they decide that killing is wrong? I mean, it's so stupid! We're powerless, too! All we had were guns and knives and shit, which are pretty fucking useless against a guy who can melt bullets before they even hit him or who can basically scald people from a few yards away. Sundew could control your freaking mind given enough time or the right conditions, and he almost got Silver Phoenix the second time! And, fuck, this was a guy who went around kidnapping and killing people! He kidnapped me! He made me kill people! He took four years of my fucking life; he doesn't *deserve* to live!

....

Sorry, sorry. I'm gonna calm down.

Fuck....

So…anyway. 'Everyone gets to live happily' and all, that's bullshit. That's the story the media and Phoenix like to tell. I mean, sure, they got snippets here and there of interviews with some of those supers that got snatched by Sundew— but only the actual notable ones, mind you. Ones like the first girl that tried to take him down were completely ignored. Not cool enough, I guess. And of course those supers are hailed for their endurance under Sundew's control and are given well-wishes and shit. Me? Nothing, except for my family once they finally found me again. And everyone at this center, of course

And, it's not like I came out of that fine, obviously. I mean, look at me, I don't have my right arm anymore! Phoenix burned it so badly that it had to be amputated, same time he screwed up this side of my face. And these scars on my left eye? Another super, and now I'm completely blind in this eye. Another one broke one of my legs and it never healed right. And aside from that stuff, I lost four years of my life. Four. Lost my job, lost my car, lost my apartment… shit, I lost my cat, too. Not to starvation, my mom thankfully had a key to my place and found him in time, but he was old. Died a year after and I didn't get to say goodbye.

But outside of my family, no one really cared or thought much about me or any of the rest of us. Not until that woman Amaya Waller sued Phoenix and the rest of the League of Superheroes for negligence 'cause of that whole vow supers make to protect the common people. I thought she was kinda crazy and that she'd never make it far with that whole case, 'cause, y'know, who gives a shit, right? But whaddya know, it made international news, even led to people in other countries doing the exact same thing. "Should superheroes take care in dispatching a supervillain's henchmen before going after the villain?", that was the title of one of the articles I saw. Lotta people saying no, lotta them saying yes. "Do minions still count as 'the common people'?" Also started to bring the whole self-defense argument into question, then revived the argument of if supers are justified in killing villains or leaving them up to the law, or if it's their duty to kill the real dangerous ones. Boy, she started a lot of shit.

Not to say I'm not glad, because I am. It was nice, actually made me not feel depressed for the first time since Sundew's arrest. And, I'll admit, I got into some shit myself, too. Started a bunch of fights online over this stuff. I know I shouldn't have, but it's hard not to start yelling at ignorant people, especially when I was already mad at everything.

That's kinda what landed me here. Watching all the debates and getting into it online just made me angrier and angrier and even more depressed. I mean, wouldn't you be when you see all these people saying that the deaths of all those people trapped like that were necessities? Or saying that a super shouldn't give a shit about your life? Or seeing people say it's my fault for trusting Sundew in the first place, or not being strong enough to resist or whatever? I know a lot of it's all bullshit and they don't know what they're talking about, but it gets to you, you know? Eventually it all just piles up. Didn't help either that I started religiously checking every news site I could every day to make sure Sundew was still locked up.

My brother got sick of it. Said he was gonna take me to get checked into a "Minion Recovery Center"—don't look at me like that, everyone calls it that—and that it'd do me a lot more good that sitting around looking for things to upset me would. My whole family kinda pushed me to it. And, here I am now, sitting here and talking to you, so you know they succeeded. It took a bit, though. Not like these places are super popular and beloved by the community, and it's not like I was out in the open with being one of Sundew's. I didn't want someone to see me or to find out where I'd disappeared to and put all the pieces together...but I was also really tired of everything.

I haven't been here for very long, but it's been alright so far. It's nice being around other people who get it, y'know? I don't have to lie and say I got caught in a housefire whenever anyone asks about what happened to me, don't have to try to come up with some bullshit excuse at job interviews for why I didn't work for four years. Can't fight with any internet assholes since I'm not allowed access to any technology. I even found some other people who got snatched by Sundew, and we'll spend hours just ragging on him and Phoenix. It's fun.

How do I feel about it all now? Right now? Well…I don't feel as guilty. By which I mean I still feel plenty guilty, but it's getting better. Still learning how to say that none of what happened or what I did was my fault and believe it. But I don't think I'll ever feel all that safe anymore knowing that Sundew's still alive out there and I almost wasn't.

Stacks

Henry Wilson

Do you have a body, or **are** you a body?
I hope you recognize this false dichotomy.
It seems that you are a phenomenon **emergent** from a body. You are
also a vector for the autonomy of ideas,
   Which themselves are emergent,
     hosted steganographically by the body,
       The littlest of modifications.
These abstruse changes to the body
   Lead to notable changes in the emergent self.
     Small changes to initial conditions
       Result in unrecognizable outcomes...

From matter,
  And time,
    There emerged life.
From life,
  And selection,
    There emerged genes.
From genes,
  And cooperation,
    There emerged organisms.
From some organisms,
  There emerged intelligence,
    There emerged agriculture,
      And society,
        And recursive language.
There emerged memes,
  Stacked on society,
    Stacked on thinking,
      Stacked on bodies,
        Stacked on genes,

>Stacked on living,
>>Stacked on matter and logic,
>>Stacked on...
>Stacked on what?

You are very high above the substrate of the world,
>Supported only by an array of abstractions,
>>Yourself an abstraction also.
>>>I invite you to look deeply down with me.

Cards

Kade Adamy

The plastic rectangles
Dealt hand to hand

The crimson hearts
The dark spades
The pale diamonds
The gloomy clubs

With the torn jack
The bent seven

The plastic paper
The smooth rectangles
Smelling of clean plastic
Stained from years of use
Twisted and bent

And only the ace of spades
Is held in any grace

As the plastic bends
And the cards wear
The sheen dulls
and the cards dealt

Little Green Forests

Nichole White

Nestled away
Comforted by the earth
Like long trees
Protects them from
The heartache of the world
A world filled with
Cockroaches

Ice Cream

Alexis Ullrich

"I don't really like ice cream all that much," Iris muttered, then immediately regretted doing so. All the other women worked with looked at her in astonishment which quickly became complete and utter disbelief, completely silent now when only seconds ago they'd been pestering her for her favorite flavor of ice cream. They'd expected her to say that she liked vanilla or chocolate or strawberry or at least say *anything*, but not *nothing*.

"You're lying!" one of them exclaimed. "There's no way!"

"You have to like some flavor," another said. "What about mint chocolate chip?"

"Cookie dough?" questioned yet another.

"Cake batter?"

"Not even vanilla? *Everyone* likes vanilla."

"Lemon? Cherry? Green tea?"

"I really don't," Iris insisted, though her voice got smaller and smaller as her cheeks turned redder and redder.

One of the older women rolled her eyes and waved Iris' words away. "What is it with kids now? Listen, you might *think* you don't like it, but I'll bet you just haven't found the right flavor yet. Trust me."

Iris did not.

She squirmed in her seat and looked between all the women, the younger of whom had stopped paying attention completely and were instead listing off stranger and stranger flavors of ice cream while the older women kept trying to convince her that she didn't know what she was talking about. Finally reaching her limit, she popped out of her seat and announced that she had to pee before running out of the room. She did not stop until she'd locked herself inside the bathroom and was sitting on top of the toilet with her head in her hands.

Stupid her. She should have said vanilla. Everyone liked vanilla, at least a little bit, and it made sense for a girl like her. It was the easy answer. Sometimes she wished it were the truth, but she really couldn't stand it. She didn't like that it was cold, she didn't like the texture, she didn't like how sticky it got when it melted, she didn't like that she had to eat it fast so it wouldn't make a huge mess...she just didn't. Couldn't. The thought of eating any made her want to gag—it always had. But she was an outlier, and she knew that very well.

Iris stayed in the bathroom for a little while longer, giving herself time to calm down from the embarrassment from before, then took another few minutes to prepare herself and get a lie together in case they asked about it again. Thankfully for her, the women had dropped the subject entirely by the time she came back, though they still gave her funny looks every now and again. She tried to pretend it didn't bother her

~

"I don't like ice cream," Iris snapped, leaning away from the spoon that her boyfriend had been sneakily moving towards her lips. "You know that."

Sean huffed and rolled his eyes. They were sitting side by side on his bed, and Iris had been trying to pay attention to the movie he'd been begging her to watch for the past few weeks. He had been working his way through a bowl of chocolate ice cream, and, apparently, coming up with some way of getting her to have some too. He always had a huge tub of it in the freezer whenever she was over at his apartment, and he ate at least one bowl every other night. He asked if she wanted some every time she was over, but usually dropped it after the second or third "no" or the first "I'm not kidding." He knew very well that she wasn't a fan of any ice cream, but that didn't stop him from trying.

"Oh sure, you say that, but have you ever even had any before?" he asked.

"Yes! And I didn't like it!"

"Yeah? What flavor?"

"Strawberry," she said, and that wasn't a lie. Once, a long time ago, she'd gotten curious about what was so great and bought a tiny cup of strawberry ice cream. She'd eaten all of it, but only because she kept hoping that maybe by the next bite it would taste better, or maybe the next one, and so on. It just wasn't for her.

Sean wiggled the spoon in front of her. "That means you haven't tried chocolate."

"It's going to start dripping on the sheets."

"How can you say you don't like it if you've never tried it?" he asked, starting to get frustrated. Then he put on a fake little pout. "Come on, Iris. Please?"

"I thought you wanted me to watch this with you," she muttered, nodding to the movie. He moved closer, still holding the spoon in front of her mouth. "We can do both."

"I don't—"

"Just a little bit? It won't hurt you."

Iris faltered and considered her options. She could say no, but she knew that if she did then he'd be pissed at her for the rest of the night, maybe even beyond that. It had happened before, and she really didn't want to end the night on a shitty note. And over ice cream? Maybe…maybe she was being dumb. It was only a little bit, after all. Just a little wouldn't be so bad…right?

"Okay," she finally said, and Sean's face lit up. He watched intently as she ate the spoonful of ice cream, and she tried not to make a face. It wasn't horrible, but it was close enough. Not to mention it had started to melt already in the spoon, so half of what she had was gross ice cream soup that was only barely cold.

All in all, it affirmed what she already knew. Great. At least it was over.

"So?" Sean asked. Iris tried for a smile.

"It was okay," she lied. Big mistake, it turned out, because then he insisted that she finish the rest with him. Apparently to him, "okay" meant "it was great" and "I want more."

"A-Actually, I didn't really—" she tried to say, but Sean wasn't listening. He had already stuck another spoonful of ice cream in her mouth, and then was insisting on another and another, and at that point she felt obligated to finish it now that she'd already started.

Later that night as they lay side-by-side, she decided that she regretted saying yes at all. A night or more of Sean being mad at her would have been better than this nasty, heavy feeling in her stomach. She didn't like ice cream. She knew she didn't, he knew she didn't. Why had he kept pushing her? Why hadn't she just gotten up and left?

And above all that, was she being stupid? It was just fucking ice cream, and yet there she was getting all worked up over it. No, it hadn't hurt her. Not in any obvious way, at least. She could put up with it, if she had to.

But…maybe that was a lie too.

The nasty feeling in her stomach stayed there for days after, and even when it was gone, she didn't feel quite right, and she didn't feel comfortable around Sean's place anymore. He tried two more times to get her to have some ice cream with him even after she admitted she hadn't actually liked it all that much, though she could tell he didn't believe her, or just wasn't listening.

Every single time he would nearly force the spoon in her mouth anyway, as if just one more taste would prove to her that she was just lying to herself.

She left him after the third time.

"I don't like ice cream," Iris said very quietly.

Quinn looked over at her. In his hands were two small tubs of ice cream, one Rocky Road and one cherry vanilla, and he'd been debating between the two when he'd asked which one she liked. She'd considered lying, but she'd been lying for a couple years now, and she liked him too much to keep it up. They'd only been seeing each other for a few weeks, Iris tiptoeing around making it official while Quinn waited for her to make up her mind. She had considered a few times just avoiding the whole ice cream thing and making a bunch of excuses for …however long she could keep it up. But she really liked Quinn, more than she'd liked anyone since Sean, and she didn't want to end up the exact same way as before, and being around Quinn she felt like she could be herself and be honest and so this was ...being herself and hoping he'd accept that, even if he didn't want to be with her anymore.

"What was that?" he asked.

"I don't like ice cream," Iris repeated, louder this time, and braced herself for the confused look, or the "You're joking, right?", or even for him to burst out laughing. For being jokingly asked what ice cream ever did to her, or being told that it was just a phase, or say he was going to show her what she was missing out on, or all the other things that had caused her to shut up about it until then.

"Oh. Okay."

Iris blinked, and then she was the one giving him the confused look. What? Was he joking? She searched his face for any sign that he was messing around with her, or maybe that he wasn't taking her seriously, but...nothing (except for a little smile when their eyes met). Maybe *he* was really good at acting, or maybe he just didn't understand.

"You ...heard *what* I said, right?" she asked.

"Yeah, and I said 'Okay'."

"Don't you think that's weird?"

He shrugged. "I mean, sure, a little. I've never met anyone who didn't like ice cream before, but, why not? My dad says I can't be his kid because I don't like apple pie—"

"You don't what?!"

"See?" he laughed. "The only thing that does bother me is that I still can't decide which one of these to buy." He contemplated the two ice creams for a moment longer, then decided to toss them both into the shopping cart. Iris was still stunned by how little it bothered him. And that he didn't like apple pie.

She hesitated. "You can't change my mind, you know. There's no special kind of ice cream that'll make me suddenly love it, in case you were thinking that."

"I wasn't. I'm guessing other people did, though."

"A couple times…You seriously don't mind?" she asked.

"Why should I? You like what you like, and you don't like what you don't like. I'm not gonna force you to eat it or anything. Besides, that means there's more for me."

Iris let out a small, relieved laugh. She wasn't completely convinced, and she'd ask him again later on just to be extra sure that he wasn't lying, and then again to make sure he hadn't changed his mind, but the idea that with him she could finally relax was enough to get her halfway there.

Quinn slipped his hand into hers and gave it a reassuring squeeze, and she could not get rid of her smile for the rest of the day.

Consistency

Stephan Pierce

They always hungry, and their clothes are worn,
No one around asked, "how may I help?"
Yet I do not mind 'cause they are warm.

I cuts daily while police gather to mourn,
But at night in the house the heat is felt.
They always hungry, and their clothes are worn,

The heats just doin' what they were sworn
To keep the area tight like a belt.
Yet I do not mind 'cause they are warm.

Last night the folks surrounded us in a swarm,
They tone was angry as they let out a yelp,
"They always hungry, and their clothes are worn,

"He cuts all our wood, consider ya'll warned."
Then theys walked on home since we'd been dealt
Yet I do not mind 'cause they are warm.

That night momma cried as I cut through storms,
Morning come: I'm cuffed, locked and withheld.
They always hungry, and their clothes are worn,
Yet I do not mind 'cause they are warm.

Hide and Seek

Jordan Bass

There's a ghost in the house, I know it. That's why I didn't want to play hide and seek, but Laura wanted to and she's older. We always do what she wants. I don't like her, but Mom gets mad when I say it.

"Danny!"

I think Laura's still downstairs. I'm in my Mom's closet, she'll never find me. I even turned off the light. I don't like it in here because of the ghost. Mom doesn't believe me, but I always hear him at night. He's got a deep voice and there are thuds on the stairs. I hear the voice in Mom's room. He sounds like Dad. She's says that I don't hear anything, but when I told Laura, she laughed at me.

"I can't tell you who that is."

"Why not?"

"You're little, and little kids don't get to know."

I told Mom Laura knows about the ghost, but she didn't believe me. "No, honey, that's not a ghost. He's my friend."

"Is it Daddy?"

"No it's not—no."

Laura won't look for me in the closet because it's dark, and I don't like the dark. It makes me throw up. Laura says I throw up too much. I don't like my nightlight either because it's for babies. I think Laura's still looking for me, because she's walking up the stairs now. She doesn't sound like the ghost. She's too quiet. Even when she's talking.

"I'm going to find you!"

I curl up more on the closet floor. The carpet is itchy. I hold out my hand in front of me, but I can't see it. I even wiggle my fingers. I don't like it. One time all the lights went out in the house while it was storming. I threw up. Dad had to clean it up and told me that the dark wasn't scary. I told him I can't breathe when it's dark, and my chest hurts.

He said, "What are you doing right now?"

I blinked at him. My mouth still tasted funny.

"You're breathing. You can still breathe in the dark, Dan."

He called me "Dan", and he only did that when he got angry. When my Mom's angry she calls me Daniel. Laura's moving around Mom's bed- room now.

"I've checked every other room, Danny. I know you're here! Just come out!"

No way. I didn't want to play, but I don't want to lose either. I don't like the word lose. Everyone sounds sad when they say it. I don't want to be in the closet because I can't see anything, and I feel sick. But I don't want to turn on the light, because then she'll find me.

"Hey, Danny, you know Mom doesn't like you in her room!"

I'm not in her room. I'm in her closet. But Mom doesn't like me in here either. It used to have a lot more clothes. A while ago I found Mom putting Dad's shirts in a garbage bag, but when I asked why, she told me to go watch TV. Th ere was a show with a talking dog on. She put the bags in the car.

"A-ha!"

Laura opens the door and it hits the wall. There's light again, and I can see the clothes and my hands and Laura at the door. I don't feel sick anymore.

"Danny, why are you hiding in the dark?"

"So, you can't find me, duh." I don't want Laura to win.

"You're scared of the dark."

"I'm not scared!"

"You throw up."

"No, I don't!"

"Oh, God, you didn't throw up, did you?" She turns on the light and

I squint.

"I don't throw up!"

"Whatever. It's my turn to hide."

"This is boring."

"You're boring."

Mom says we argue too much, but she's downstairs. I hear her talking on the phone. She sounds angry, but she uses the word frustrated. I can't say it well yet. The doorbell rings and Laura jumps. I stand up. I think Laura wants to go get the door, and Mom says she isn't old enough yet, but Laura wants to do it anyway.

"I'm coming, just a second," Mom calls.

"Come on," Laura says. She pulls me towards the stairs. I don't want to see who it is. Mom says I shouldn't like strangers. Mom opens the door. I don't see who it is, but I hear the deep voice. It's the ghost, it has to be. I move backwards. Laura doesn't look scared, and she can see him. Laura turns to look at me.

"What's up with you?"

"That's the ghost."

Laura snorted, like a goat. "You should go meet him."

"I don't want to."

"Why not?"

"I don't know."

"Are you scared of him? Dude, he's not a ghost. I was messing with you. He's a friend of Mom's."

"Okay."

"You can't be scared of everything forever. You have to go see him. He's not a ghost, I promise."

"It's not Dad."

"It's ...no. Dad's not a ghost. Come on, Danny."

I go down the stairs behind Laura. She's faster than me. When I'm at the bottom, Mom looks happy to see me. She's with the man with the voice. He's tall and has black hair, and he doesn't look like Dad. He doesn't look like a ghost either. I don't like him. He stops talking to Mom and looks at me.

"Hey, kid. You're Danny, right? Your Mom's told me all about you." Mom wants me to answer. I don't answer. Mom says sorry.

"He told me he thought you were a ghost. You must have heard us after you were in bed, right, honey? This is my friend William."

William bends down and smiles at me. I don't like his face. Mom keeps talking. "He's…he's been having trouble adjusting to the new situation. William's nice, honey. I promise."

I don't believe her. I don't want to be nice to William. I would've liked a ghost better. He has the ghost's voice, and I thought it sounded like Dad, but it doesn't, and it's not a ghost either. I run back upstairs. Laura yells after me for being rude. Mom says sorry again, but not to me. I go back upstairs into the closet in Mom's room and shut the door. Laura couldn't find me for forever, so let Mom try to find me now. I dare her. I turn the light off again, just to be sure I'm hidden. No ghost will find me now. My chest hurts. I throw up on her carpet. No one comes to clean it up.

Dormant Thoughts

Liam McLaurin

I stand to the side
Watching my friend stress and cry
But what can I do?

She's a volcano
Dormant, but waiting to burst;
And so I must help.

Dormant volcano,
You drive yourself to water,
Waiting to erupt.

Flame leaps from your eyes
Seeking to sear land and sky.
I dip low to you:

"Speak your woes to me,
Great mountain of fire— my friend—
What harms you so much?"

Your power erupts,
Bones of rock splinter and crack,
Magma makes you smile.

"I seek cold water,
My fires burn too deep and hot.
They will scorch my friends."

"My friend, be at ease.
You seek death too easily,
Which I can't allow."

With a gentle palm,
I caress your flaming head
And dispel your worries.

First Date

Lacey Beamer

"Do you wanna get some gyros?" he asks. Except he says it "guy rows," like he wants to go to the river and find some frat boys on boats rented from Friends of the Rappahannock. The kind of boys that live off Natty Lites and Instagram likes on pictures of fish hanging from the mouths.

"It's gyro," I correct with practiced ethnicity. The "r" tries to roll on my tongue, but it only teeters, rocking back and forth slightly. "Year- oh. Hero, even," I add slowly.

Guy Row Polo Shirt shrugs. "Tomato, to-mah-to." He's got that douche-y smirk on his face, the kind that would maybe be more impressive if it weren't for the few stringy hairs attached limply to his upper lip. I wonder if he'd care about the difference if I threw a tomato in his face.

Mom will say I'm being picky again, as if this is as simple as ice cream flavors or as if Guy Row Polo Shirt is even worth sampling. Maybe he'd be tomato flavored.

Yiayia will understand, though. She'd call him the frog before the prince. The frogs from her past sound a lot better than mine, though, admiring her under stained glass windows and dancing round the room in the Kalamatianos. She loves to dance, but she doesn't anymore. Too many hip and knee replacements, and no one to dance with, anymore.

On the phone last week she told me she barely looked twice at Pappou before he asked her for a dance. "Two left feet," she said, and a bad knee of his own. But she danced with him anyway. He was her frog and the prince.

I frown at Guy Row Polo Shirt. It's a nice polo shirt-new, and my favorite shade of blue.

"Okay," I answer.

Wishbone

Jordan Bass

"So, you actually cheated on her?"

The gunshot echoed into the forest, coming nowhere near the tree with the haphazard paper target taped to it. Jonah ground his teeth, readying the pistol for reload. He glared at his sister, who was sitting beside him on the chilled ground, jeans slowly becoming damp.

"No, dude! She just keeps telling people that. And no one in school believes me. I have the receipts!"

"Sure."

"I'm serious. My phone broke."

"That's convenient."

"Who's the one with the gun?"

Sarah snorted. "Try hitting something and then I'll be scared."

"The targets off."

"Excuses, excuses." Sarah stumbled through the leaves ten feet ahead to the tree, predictably free of bullet marks. The fall foliage created natural knee-deep leaf piles, so it was no surprise when Sarah tripped on her hands and knees, scraping her fingers through the dry forest floor.

"You good?" Jonah didn't sound too concerned, still fiddling with reloading the gun. They had taken it from their father's sock drawer, the second most obvious place he could have hidden it. The first most obvious place was on the top shelf of the master room closet. The Christmas presents were hiding under the bottom shelf, and Sarah and Jonah's Father wasn't too happy when they went crawling under the shelf five years back. The gun case fell to the floor, all sleek and black, like a secret agent. Jonah, twelve at the time, took out the gun while Sarah stared, wide-eyed at the thing she knew from the loud noises on TV. She screamed for her Father, and the gun remained in the sock drawer from then on. Jonah found it two days later, snooping around for loose change. He didn't tell Sarah about it until he decided she was old enough, when she stopped being so annoying and rolling her eyes so much.

They still annoy each other to no end, but sometimes they try and shoot the gun.

Sarah slipped in the leaves, attempting to push herself back up. "I dunno, she said you cheated on her."

"You talked to her?" Jonah had finally managed to reload the bullets, but lost interest as soon as the task was complete. He clicked on the safety.

"Kind of, she said—ow!" Sarah withdrew her hand quickly from the mess of brown leaves, only to see them being spotted with blood. She glanced at her hand, now presenting a small scrape across it, already clotting up like a papercut.

"She said what?" Jonah was putting the gun back in the case now, brushing off any leaf fragments, closing it firmly. Dad would never know. He'd just have to replace the bullets.

"I just got cut!" Sarah finally pushed herself up on the tree, presenting her hand to her brother. He looked on in disbelief.

"You cut yourself on a leaf?"

"Yeah, dipshit."

Jonah had picked up the habit of rolling his eyes. He carefully slid over to the tree, his arms out slightly to keep his balance, a warm blue jacket blanketing his torso, and some of his legs too. Jonah would never admit that he was shorter than his younger sister, even though it was almost obvious at this point.

"You can't curse like that, Dad'll end you."

"He doesn't care when you do it."

"I'm the *provider* of the household."

Sarah snorted at the old joke. At fifteen and just discovering opinions, she realized she didn't agree with her Father on anything, almost to the point of wishing for her mother back. After all, she left for a reason.

Her father called it "going through a *phase.*" *Phase* was always drawn out, as if by the time he finished the word she would be a changed woman. Unfortunately for him, she still wanted to dye her hair. As a young and wild youth, she realized she must retaliate. Her father's constant and only answer to why, why did she have to unload the dishwasher or sweep the porch or get him a beer, was "I'm the provider of the household." Right, the *providerrrrrrrrr*. She drew out the world, hoping to make a point, but instead just led to her brother picking up the phrase as well. Unless they're out in the woods, that's really the only thing he says to her.

Jonah tore down the bullet-less target, stuffing the paper in his coat pocket.

"Seriously, what did she say?"

"Mostly that she didn't want to talk about it." Sarah was back on the ground, digging through the leaves.

"That's it?"

"Well, yeah. That and that you cheated on her."

"I didn't—"

"Found it!" Sarah triumphantly pulled a long, thin, white object out of the camouflage of the leaves, all jagged edges and twisted sides. She brandished it like a sword. Jonah stared at her, shocked into silence. "It cut me," Sarah explained. "You know, the perpetrator. The—I think it's a bone?"

"It looks like some weird shit from *Operation*."

"Oh, so a bone then?"

"Shut up, you know what I mean." Jonah held out his hand towards her, hesitating to touch the offensive, pointy, still-unknown- to-him object. Their father had tried to take Jonah hunting a few times throughout the years, which only ended in disappointment. He had wanted to find a good buck and hang its head on the wall. Jonah had silently thought that would look tacky, but it's not like he could shoot anything anyway. Every time Jonah shot and hit some patch of leaves in the distance, his father would scowl at him. He only smiled when they were hunting when Jonah talked about his girlfriend.

"I think it's a wishbone."

"Based on what, your extensive medical knowledge?" Jonah withdrew his hands, stuffing them in his pockets, staring at the bone. "Wait, do you think it's a human?"

"What? No! No?" Sarah suddenly seemed much more uncomfortable, propping the bone up against the tree. "Uh, maybe?"

"You know what bones look human? Deer bones. Bear bones. Anything with bones that's close to human size."

"It could totally be human."

"Skull or it didn't happen."

"That is so stupid—"

"Seriously, what did she say to you? Because I didn't cheat on her."

"Oh my God, you're still on that?"

"Her friends are all DM'ing me on Instagram. It's a mess.

"Seriously?"

"Yeah."

Sarah was quiet for a minute. "She said to tell you that you're the worst. And that she wanted to know the other girl's name."

"There isn't one."

When Sarah didn't respond, Jonah looked away and continued. "I didn't know how to end it with her, and she was always accusing me of cheating and stuff, until I just stopped saying I didn't cheat. I never actually cheated. So, stop saying it."

"You're not gonna tell her you didn't cheat?"

"What does it matter? Relationship over, I'm a free man. Women are the worst."

"But everyone thinks…"

"What do I care?"

Sarah pulled up the mysterious possibly-human bone and taps it against the tree.

"Okay, you pull on one end, I pull on the other."

Jonah didn't move to take the other side of the bone, instead rolling his eyes and turning to collect the gun case. Sarah bit her lip.

"I will actually pay you, I'm serious."

The gun case was forgotten. Jonah kicked through the leaves, back to Sarah's side.

"What is it?"

"It's a wishbone, right? Like a Thanksgiving thing. You pull on one end, and I pull on the other, and if you win, I'll give you five bucks."

"Fine-."

"But if I win," Sarah continued, much louder, "You have to go to your ex and tell her to leave you alone because she's insane."

Jonah pushed back his dark hair. "Isn't a bone supposed to be stronger than steel?"

"Sure," Sarah grinned. "That's how you broke your arm, right? Hitting it with steel. Not jumping off a swing set."

Jonah grumbled as he grabbed the other end of the bone. "I was five."

"Yeah, and I was three and I still remember how stupid it was. Okay, one, two—."

The bone snapping was almost louder than the gunshot. The next day, Sarah and Jonah were ignoring each other at school, following the mandatory family "don't talk to me until 3pm" rule. Jonah followed his ex to her class and called for her to wait. She didn't look any different from usual, face void of most expression besides the pursed lips. Tacky. Quickly, before either of them could run off, he pulled his half of the forest bone out of his backpack and handed it to her.

"I didn't cheat on you," he announced, loudly. "But we should break up anyway." He walked off in the opposite direction, leaving the proof of his completed bet with his ex. She looked down at the bone fragment, disgusted.

"What am I supposed to do with this?"

Dinner at Eight

Regan Flieg

Fingers fumble around the metal loops of chain. With eyes fixed in sharp focus on the two necklaces, I can almost forget the hands frantically untangling them are mine. He'll be home in twenty minutes and if the table isn't set, he'll be angry. He'll throw the tall glass vase filled with delicate and blameless flowers, sending it to shatter against the dining room wall, just barely missing the cold, abstract painting that will loom over us through dinner.

I could back out now. He will never know I even tried.

But he will notice if the necklace is missing, the one he gave me as a present after his trip to a city with lights bigger and brighter and bolder than mine. He will see it's missing and think I am ungrateful. He will be angry, but he can't suspect a thing.

Mother will be disappointed when they tell her what has happened, what I have done. But my ghost will whisper softly that we were the tangled chains of necklaces and trying to pry us apart only made my fingers bleed.

I will stand by this choice: till death do us part.

7:46. The kitchen timer blares. Soon, he will swing open the front door, and I will try not to wish he would call to me, sing-song and cheery, a "Honey, I'm home" like my father in my youth. It would only make it harder. He has never called me Honey. He has hardly called me Marcy or even Mrs. Nelson, and I wonder what our tombstones will say or if they'll bury us together when they discover the truth. Will they lay us side by side, cold and stiff and silent as we've always been in life? Or will we be released, one thin gold chain slipping loose from the other?

Onions are the Enemy

Abigail Bruce

"You'll have the whole place to yourself since Kent and David will be at camp."

Spending a week with Oma and Opa wasn't bad, but compared with summer baseball camp, it was less exciting. It's no fair I can't go. Stupid all boys rule.

"You can watch TV, play in the yard, and ride your bike if Oma is in a good mood. But stay out of the garden."

"Helga you mean," I said. My mom pressed her lips together. Uh-oh- oh, I think that was the wrong thing to say.

"That is not how you address her."

"But if that is her name, why can't I call her that?"

My mother pressed her lips tighter, they were turning white. "Because it is more respectful for you to call her Oma young lady." Young lady? Yep, I blew it. I slumped back in my seat and leaned against the car window. I twirled my short brown hair between my fingers to help me not to talk anymore. My dad in the driver's seat chuckled. He shared my mom's view on how to respectfully talk to people, but he thought it was funny when my mother was flustered by small things.

Why couldn't I keep my big mouth shut? I don't understand why I can't call them by their names. They call me by my name, why couldn't I call Opa and Opa Helga and Donald? When I heard mom talk on the phone, I asked who Donald was and she said it was my Opa. I was so confused, Donald was Opa? I was like I had never known them. Not that I don't love them anymore, but I felt foolish for not knowing about it. If only I had asked sooner.

I watched the matching houses of my grandparents neighborhood as they whizzed by. First floor houses with no upstairs to run up and down. Not many homes with other kids, just older couples and military families that wouldn't stay long. We passed the house with the large Steelers flag which meant after two more left turns we would be there.

We pulled up the front of the one-story house with pale blue walls, black roof, and an iron horseshoe the size of my head hanging next to the front door just above the rusted mailbox. It was the only house here that had a wooden front porch. Dad said that he and my uncle had built it for Oma and Opa so they could sit outside and smoke. My dad parallel parked in one motion, clicked the lever, and the engine cut off. Likewise, I unbuckled my seatbelt, pulled the door latch, and was out of the car.

They were already waiting on the porch as I skipped up the concrete path. They were a matching set. A king and queen sitting above the ground about to watch knights joust. Oma was relaxing in her long red floral dress that draped over her plump form. Opa wore his usual black suspenders and crisp light blue button up shirt that was always neatly tucked in. I leaped up the three brick steps in one bound and made a crash landing into my Oma's outstretched arm. She squeezed me and started into her usual greeting.

"Ah my Heidi, look how big you are getting. A vat is dis? Anoder bruise? Why you play so ruff for? Leave dat baseball to those boys. Ah, my little soldier, can't help yourself can you?" Another squeeze and she released me, leaning the side of her face to me, pointing to her cheek. I planted the expected kiss on her cheek and stepped back, holding onto the chair's arm as I balanced on my heels.

"Where's mine?"

Opa folded his hands in his lap and frowning as he looked away towards the neighbor's house. This was our custom. He would act offended that I didn't say hello to him first, knowing how upset Oma would get if she didn't receive her hug first. His face would not change, but his bottom lip would pout out, showing his hurt. I placed my feet back on the ground and wound around Oma to stand next to him. He was still looking away from me, but I could see a little smirk through his white whiskers. Calmly, I placed my hands on his rough calloused hands and leaned in to kiss his cheek. He would chuckle and pat my hands, his way of giving a hug, and our greeting was done. Opa was softer in his greetings compared with Oma, but I didn't mind, it was something that we did.

Mom and dad caught up with us on the porch, repeating the same greeting, hugs and handshakes. Instructions were given for my care that my Oma brushed off with a huff, I was told to behave, one more round of hugs, waves goodbye, and then my parents drove off.

We sat on the porch a little while longer as me and Oma carried on about this and that. Opa nodding his head every now and then, with the occasional comment. He rubbed the scar on his left arm, the one I was scared to ask about. Opa wasn't a chatterbox like me. That's what mom and dad called me, I had too much in me to keep to myself, so I just let it all out. Opa was different, he was a listener. He took in every-thing you said, chewed on it, and gave it back to you in one sentence. I remember watching a National Geographic about lions being able to roar so loud that they could stun prey right in front of them. That was nothing compared to what Opa could do, he could stun a lion with one word.

Being around him helped me to keep words from falling out of me. He didn't speak often so it was a treat to hear his voice. His presence made you want to be quieter, careful not to make too much noise. It made you pay attention to your surroundings. Sometimes it made me nervous how quiet he could be. I wasn't sure what was going through his mind or where I stood with him. Oma told me that was just his way. Some people talked, others listened. You had to pay attention, watch how he acted, watch what his face did. I found that his lips and cheeks were the best way to tell his mood. Usually people say look at their eyes, but his were blurred and magnified behind his thick glasses. When he moved his mouth, it made his Santa Claus beard wiggle, making it simple for me to keep track of his thoughts.

Oma stamped out the stump of her cigarette and checked her watch and said it was 12:10, according to her we were late for lunch. We shuffled our way inside and were greeted with arctic air conditioning and the faint smell of wood lacquer. I ran around the tight hall's corner and took my place in the breakfast nook, sliding along the booth seat cushion close to the window and to the left of the small television set. Opa settled himself into in his chair, directly in front of TV to watch the cop show he liked that I could never remember the name of. Oma brought out cold cut sandwiches overfilled with lunchmeat and tomatoes, a side of Lays potato chips, followed with a large glass of milk. We gave thanks and I was told I couldn't play outside until the plate was clean and the milk gone. I hated to drink milk; it took too long to finish it. Oma had fussed I couldn't grow without it, that my bones would break if I didn't drink it all. I had fallen many times and my bones seemed okay afterwards. It wasn't until Opa told me that milk would help me to run faster to steal bases during baseball that I forced myself to keep the milk down with bites of the sandwich.

I finished my meal and Opa nodded to Oma, granting permission for me to leave the table. I was given the usual set of instructions from Oma: "Have fun, don't go in the garden, don't touch the tools, come and get water if I need it, don't get too dirty, and stay out of Opa's garden." I pulled back the plastic tan curtain and opened the glass sliding door that led to the backyard, having to use my full weight to make the mechanism grudgingly slide open.

Everyone took every chance to tell me to stay out of the garden, not that I ever did. I liked to walk by it, looked around at what was inside, but I wasn't stupid enough to go in. The infamous garden was protected by chicken wire and a white fence. Clearly stating that viewers were to mind the border or there were consequences to the trespasser who did not listen. Opa was clear with his limits. When he set a rule, you better listen. If he was willing to tell you, he thought you didn't know. If you got caught, you didn't have an excuse that he didn't warn you. He told you once, that should be enough. Opa had told me one time to stay out of his garden, so I did.

I was just tall enough that I could see over the pointed fence posts that came up to Opa's waist. The ground beneath the plants was darker and the tops of the leaves glistened under the hot sun.

Opa must have watered them earlier now that it was getting hot again. I loved the way the garden smelled after he watered everything, like the smell after it rains. Opa's hands would smell like mud afterwards and Oma would fuss at him to wash his hands and arms before he came in.

I walked my usual tour around the garden fence, keeping an arm's length distance in case someone caught a glance from the back door and thought I was getting too curious. The garden was set up in six even rectangle shapes, plots Opa had called them. There were two feet between the rows of plants so that you could walk and work between them. Vegetables grew in the three plots to the left, closer to the slanted greenhouse attached to the car garage. The three plots to the right along the wood fence were an assortment of flowers and blooming bushes. Cucumbers, peppers, and baseball sized tomatoes strung like Christmas lights along the wood poles Opa placed to keep them from falling over. Opa had moved the veggies from the right side of the yard because when they grew close to the fence, the neighbor had reached through the gaps in the wood posts and stolen entire vines of plants. The neighbor said he didn't do it, but Opa took no chances and planted a bush that stabs you if you got too close. You couldn't even pull off a leaf to rip it up without drawing blood.

I didn't know all the names of the colorful flowers that he plant-ed, but I loved to look at them and guess their names. I would call out to Opa as he worked and would be answered with a nod shaking yes or no. My last victory was the chrysanthemum bush which took me two weeks to guess. I cheated and look in a book at the library. Opa nodded yes and it was on to the next plant to guess.

I didn't understand how he could make all these plants grow. They were all different and looked hard to take care of. I had killed the three daisy buds he had given me to care for. I couldn't get anything to grow, but Opa could. I watched as the breeze made the vegetables swing on their vines and wondered why Opa would do something that took so much work. How did he remember everything you needed to do to keep these plants alive? Why keep at it? I wanted to know why, what did he do this all for? Questions that didn't used to bother me before started coming up like burps that need to be released. But I couldn't ask Opa.

Opa's garden was like his life. I saw it right in front of me but didn't know a thing about it. It was right there with all the answers, but I wasn't allowed in. It wasn't my garden to disturb and dig up, I could only watch and hope to find the answers.

I completed my second loop in front of the fence, pausing in front of the flower side of the garden. Opa must have taken out some flowers in the middle of the three plots on the flower side because the Irises and Daffodils were gone and a row of five highlighter pink Tulips were in their place. I wish he would have planted the yellow or purple ones, but maybe he couldn't control the color. I guess they looked nice. But there was something weird growing between the two tulips in the middle. Maybe it was a baby tulip? But it didn't look the same as the others. A thin, pale green stalk that looked sick compared to the thick- er darker green stems. Where had I seen it before? In the woods? The park? Or was it at the field by the school that the science teacher took us to look at wild plants? Yes, that was it, but what was the name of it? Oh right, wild onions.

But Opa hated onions. He never, ever ate them. No matter how many times Oma tried to sneak them into the food she made he would taste her trickery and spit it out. Did Opa know it was here? Maybe I should go tell him? I started walking toward the house and grabbed the handle, ready to slide open the door. Maybe I should wait? I had just come outside and Opa would still be watching his show and wouldn't want to be disturbed. I turned back to the garden that Opa worked so hard to keep, worked so hard to keep the plants healthy. He shouldn't have to work so hard without any help. I carefully approached the white gate protecting the garden and rested my shaking hand on the black iron latch, as if it was an electric fence. The air around the gate smelled of toothpaste from the mint plants Opa grew along the fence to keep the critters out. I looked back at the glass sliding door, the curtains were still pulled, I was safe for now. I lifted the latch and slowly pushed open the gate and felt like Alice entering into a strange new world. The garden looked different than the hundreds of times I peeked over the fence. It seemed to breath in and out with the breeze.

Stay out of Opa' s garden.

I paused midstep. This was the farthest I had been in the garden. I had never even passed the post, but the warning echoed in me. Alarms with spinning lights frantically telling me not to be stupid. I looked up and saw the plot with tulips and found the intruder, waving his thin, green onion stalks at me, mocking my cowardness. Oh no, not in Opa's garden! But I could get the onion out, he didn't have to know.

I took a gulp and stomped my foot down, forcing my body to move forward. I stumbled forward across the unfamiliar path that Opa had worn down with his steps during his routine. I walked by the vegetable Christmas lights and carefully sat down in front of the tulips, confronting the invader. I slapped my hands down around the onion, closing off his escape routes. Nowhere for it to run to now. The onion shook, it knew it was doomed. Now how to get it out?

I looked around the garden for the short shovel thing that Opa used to dig up and catapult weeds out of the ground. There were no tools around, I should have known, Opa put them all neatly away when he was done. I had seen him use his hands sometimes when he didn't have a tool. I made my fingers straight like I had seen Opa do and plunged them into the earth around the onion, like those big construction diggers, and scooped out the trespasser. It felt good to send the stinky onion flying across the garden. Now to hide the evidence. I started to push the dirt back to fill the hole when there was a glisten of something white in the dark ground. I dug around the white form only to find not one, but about six other onion balls. It was an invasion. Is this why Opa worked so hard every day, because he was being attacked from all sides? I sat back and took in the garden, it seemed so much bigger, the life growing here felt intimidating. Opa was fighting a battle this whole time, without any help, never complaining, all while I was playing and bothering with names of plants. Is that why he looked sad those times when I caught him staring off at a wall, looking at the pictures relatives I never knew?

Why didn't he ask for help? He could ask Oma, ask Mom and Dad, David, Kent, me, but he didn't. He kept it to himself, like he kept his past to himself. I picked out the white onion and tossed it between my hands like a baseball. Would he be embarrassed that I found all these onions that he had missed? Angry? I set the onion on the ground beside me and looked at the work before me. He shouldn't be embarrassed, he won't have to ask me, I'll help him.

I rolled up my imaginary sleeves the way Opa did before he started working and threw my hands into the dirt to destroy the enemy. It was getting hot and my sweat rolled off my elbows, but I can't stop now, there was work to be done. The onions smelled strange, sweet and gross at the same time like the beer Opa drank. Opa told me I wouldn't like beer and that I shouldn't want to drink it. I was nervous to ask why, but said yes to not touch it. He only drank one beer a day, telling Oma before he opened it. I would sometimes see her later counting the cans in the fridge and writing down notes on a pad of paper by the fridge. He only drank more than one when his siblings, my great aunts and uncles, came to visit and brought a full wine bar. They would tease him that he couldn't hold his liquor like he used to and get him to drink until he started giggling. That was when Oma would call for my parents to come get me and my brothers. The next day Opa wouldn't look us in the eyes and say over and over that he was sorry. I hated when they came.

Another onion gone. A small pile of baseball sized onions was growing taller as I ripped more and more of their fallen brothers out of the ground. Opa will be proud that I got the intruders out of his gar- den, taking up space that was meant for the real plants. These weeds wouldn't grow up and choke the veggies he would collect and can as they were ready. Opa always made sure there was food in the cupboard, either from his garden or the food from the store. I once asked him if we would be able to eat the wall of endless cucumbers and tomatoes.

"You never want to be hungry, it's worse than death." he had said. I asked Oma the reason for all the food and she had told me that Opa had grown up in a big family during the Depression and didn't want to live like that ever again. I tried to think of what would make. Opa so sad that he had to have food to make him feel better. It must have been bad if he had to make eighteen jars of green beans.

I was panting and my hair stuck to my face and neck, but there were no more onions. It was done, the garden was free. Opa would have one less thing to worry about today. He would see that I stopped the invasion, single handedly, and freed the new tulips from the wild onions. Maybe he would let me come in and help him. He wouldn't have to be alone in his fight. He could trust me with his secrets, his past, his story. I scooped together the loose dirt and pushed and patted it until it looked like how I found it. I stood up and shook the dirt off my hands and right leg that had gone numb, admiring my work. Now to get rid of the intruders.

"What is this?"

I jumped and landed on my numb leg, losing my balance and falling face first onto the pile of dirt I had just put back. He said it so quietly, but the roar of obvious anger scared me so that I froze on the ground and I started to shake. I was caught. I was caught by Opa. He had appeared out of nowhere and was standing in the open gate with his arms crossed. The sunlight hit him from behind blocking the top of his face. I could see his lips tighten in a frown and he tapped his fingers on his arm, waiting for an explanation.

"I-I'm so-r-rry. I was just tryin t-to help ...you." My words sounded like a deflating balloon. I picked myself off the ground, rubbing my right shoulder that I had fallen on.

"You know you are not supposed to be here." The quiet rumble of his words shook lose the handles of a water faucet that were filling my eyes with water. I didn't want to cry, I hated crying. But my eyes were starting to leak and a warm lump choked my throat.

"But ...there wer-re onions."

Opa tilted his head slightly to the left. "Excuse me?"

I pointed to my evidence piled neatly on the ground. "See, they were in the ground ...and ...and ...I saw the green stem, like ...like the wild, on-oni-on teacher had shown us. And ...yo-you don't like onions and you work so hard I ... I ... know you hate th-the-them. I just wwa-wanted to help. I wanted to he-he-help you. I ...I ...I'm ...s-s-ssorry. I'm sorry..." I was hiccuping so hard it hurt my chest and globs of snot were sliding out of my nose. Opa was gonna be mad, he was gonna be so mad. He won't let me sit with him, he won't talk to me anymore, he won't tell me the names of the plants, he won't let me come over, he won't ever greet me again. After this, there would be only silence.

Opa started laughing. Deep chuckles and loud gasps of breath were bursting out of his mouth, very loudly. He placed a hand on his face and one around his waist as his laughter got louder, I think he was starting to cry. I had never heard him this loud before. I didn't like it, what was he gonna do? I can't see his cheeks. He paused a moment, taking deep breaths, and pointed at the pile. "Those are tulip bulbs, not onions."

Huh? Bulbs. Oh no. I had never seen one before but Opa had said flower bulbs were fancy flower seeds that were different from vegetable seeds. I didn't know. I didn't know, now he knows I don't know. I could feel my face getting hotter, burning as cold tears continued to escape my eyes. Stupid, stupid, stupid! I closed my eyes and tried to make myself invisible. I wanted to run from the garden and never have to see those stupid fake onions again.

"Well, are you gonna clean up this mess?"

I peeked open my eyes and sucked up the snot still coming out of my nose. I looked at Opa confused. Why wasn't he yelling? Opa walked to the slanted greenhouse and pulled a keyring from his pocket, found the key he needed, and unlocked the door. He disappeared into the greenhouse and came out with the small shovel thing in his hand, closing the door behind him. "No TV for the rest of the week." He was still wiping tears, trying to catch his breath. He stood next to me and got on his knees in front of the tulips. He held the shovel towards me, "You got them out, you put them back."

I was confused, I think I was in trouble. I broke the rule, the big rule, where was my punishment? I sniffled and looked at Opa, scrunching my eyebrows. Opa held it out closer to me but it seemed like a trap. When adults tell you you aren't in trouble, but you really are. I kept my hands to my sides. Opa shrugged and said, "Well, if you don't want to help...."

"I do, I do." I snatched the shovel thing from his hand and sat on the ground. I started digging up the ground just like I had found it. Opa said nothing as I frantically threw dirt around, but would put his hand on mine and showed me the "right" way to dig the dirt, how to gently place the bulbs back in the ground, not drop them in. We worked in silence until I had finished putting the flower bulbs back in their home. Opa clapped the dirt from his hands and I did the same. We sat on the ground for awhile, not talking, not looking at one another, but watched as the wind made the plants bob and weave.

"When did you get that scar, the one on your left arm?" Opa rubbed his arm and looked at the fence of the thieving neighbor, his lips parted and then closed. He opened them again and said, "Before I met your Oma."

~

"Mom. It's too hot. Can I please go back inside?"

"If you want them to finish growing before you go back to school you better finish planting the last two."

Ethan groaned but considered what I had said. I handed him the spade and he placed the last two tomato plants into the ground. He wiped his forehead with his arm and picked up the spade to join me at the gate.

"See, now it is all done." I said.

Ethan looked back at the tomato plants, just vines now, but they soon would wind their way up the wood post and drop plum tomatoes. Ethan closed the gate behind us as we left the garden, smiling at his handy work. "Thanks for letting me help you." he said.

"Well, I thought it was about time."

"And you're not mad?" I stopped to look back at Ethan. He ducked his head and met my eyes; silently pleading he be grounded and not given a spanking.

"I am. But don't worry, you'll pay me back."

Ethan seemed relieved at this answer, but made a face of suspicion as to what punishment I meant. We walked back up to the house, washing the dirt off of our hands and legs with the hose before sitting on the back porch to dry off. It was just past three in the afternoon and the sun was blazing overhead, another reason I wanted to have the planting done earlier. But catching Ethan digging up rocks to build an irrigation ditch to water the plants had set back my

" Hey Mom." Ethan said.

"Mhm." I said.

"How come you know so much about plants and stuff?"

"I'll tell you about it sometime."

Ronald McDonald as My Witness

Jordan Beamer

A lukewarm McDonald's bag sat between us. I picture a greasy, salty stain on the wooden bench, remnants of the cholesterol trap of two large fries. If only Zeke knew the fourth date is when I cannot help noticing what qualities my brain catalogues as wrong.

For example, his eyes seem blue, but if I look too long, they appear glassy and greyish. And if l look down, I see a zit under his nose he must have picked at, because it's bulging, angry, and red. Even further down on his face is a tiny cut on the comer of his lip, and I wonder if he got it shaving, because I have never seen Zeke without his dark hair slicked and gelled and a clean-shaven face.

Then he says "Nikki," and I look down at his hands, imagining them on my waist, or worse, in my hair, spreading salt and fryer grease from the fries. He could have licked salt off his fingers, and my stomach cringes at the thought of saliva from his fingertips in my hair. I remember that in a matter of seconds, he might put his mouth on mine, and I would be exposed to him. What if leftover salt on my lip seeped into his cut? Or I open my eyes and see his acne reaching to infect my face?

Zeke moves the bag aside with one hand and slides closer. I think of slimy hands, an unclean face, compromised lip, and grease resting on the wood that will stain his shorts if he comes any closer. He leans in. I shove my hand into the soggy bag, and with Ronald McDonald as my witness, I force four french-fries into his mouth. He jolts, and I know the salt has touched his wound.

Pantoum of Judith

Kendall Cole

What did Judith feel that night?
As she held Holofernes down
And ripped through his flesh
Holding the gilded hilt of a dagger

As she held Holofernes down
Gripping his hair in her delicate hand
Holding the gilded hilt of a dagger
And tore his head from his drunken body

Gripping his hair in her delicate hand
Did she feel fear or revulsion?
Tearing his head from his drunken body
"The Lord has struck him down by the hand of a woman."

Did she feel fear or revulsion?
When his blood spurted into her breast and she cried
"The Lord has struck him down by the hand of a woman."
What did Judith feel that night?

Just a Glance

Alexis Ullrich

Orpheus didn't look back, but Eurydice did. As she followed him back through the underworld's throat, she turned her eyes to the darkness they were leaving behind. How far had they gone up the tunnel? How quickly would she be able to run back and beg Hades to let her stay before Orpheus reached the surface?

She looked again at Orpheus—or, rather, at his back. That was all she was allowed to see, and he was allowed none of her. If he turned to look before they reached the surface, even just a quick, tiny glance, she would be pulled back into the realm of the dead. A small, small part of her hoped he would stay vigilant. The rest hoped that he would not.

Beyond Orpheus was a pinprick of light. It was the exit out of Hades, the return to the land of the living. Once he crossed the thresh- old, she would be alive again, free to walk the earth as she pleased. She did not want to be, because being dead meant the end to all the troubles of the living. In Elysium, everything had been peaceful, and she had wanted for nothing, save for her husband. Alive....

She imagined a man standing at the mouth of the tunnel. He had dark hair, a strong build, and a deceptively kind smile that made her stomach lurch. When she exited the tunnel, she imagined that he would grab her roughly, renewing the bruises on her arms. Orpheus would not be with her, just like before.

Eurydice hugged herself and shut her eyes. One deep breath, then another and another, until she had managed to calm down. Aristaeus wouldn't be there, she told herself, and even if he was, Orpheus was with her this time. He wouldn't let anything happen to her, not after what he'd gone through to get her back.

But how long would that last?

When she opened her eyes, the exit had gotten closer, but there was still time. She chewed her lip, then opened her mouth to speak, but hesitated before any sound could come out. Duty and desire stopped her. Duty as a wife, because as a wife should she not return to her husband? He had come to get her, and few people were ever given second chances at life, so how could she say no? And she did want to be with him, she did. She had missed him so, so much since her death. Well, there he was, leading her back to the place where they could be together. She should have been happy, or at least pretended to be.

But... she hadn't been truly happy for a long time, not until she'd died. When she had heard that Orpheus had come to take her back to the surface, the happiness she'd had in death wilted in her hands.

Not so long ago, she would have given the world for Orpheus. She would have done absolutely anything for him, so wrapped up in him as she was. She had even dismissed Hymen's warning that they would not live happily forever, even though she knew better than to ignore the words of a god. She was in love, and that was more powerful. Everything had been perfect.

Then she'd caught Aristaeus' eye. It was just a glance, a smile and nod by way of greeting, and that was all. She had not meant to attract him, not at all, but it had been done, and he would not leave her alone afterwards.

Thing between them had started innocently enough, with nothing more than a simple "hello" passing between them in the mornings and a "goodnight" in the evenings. She would smile when she saw him, and that must have encouraged him, because soon enough he began to approach her to start up conversations. He would jump whenever she needed help and was at her side within seconds, so long as Orpheus wasn't around. He began to endlessly compliment her as well, always focusing on how beautiful she was. It was obvious that he'd had feelings for her, but it was also obvious that she was married. She even told him that directly as soon as she realized his intentions. He, so it turned out, did not care.

He started to turn up wherever she was, sometimes only watching her from afar. He would even show up to watch the nymphs dance, though the location of these dances was rarely ever the same. His compliments became more obscene, travelling from her face and down her body. When she was alone, she was sure she could still feel his eyes on her. She was certain these were no coincidences; he was following her, and she did not think there was anything innocent about him anymore.

She had tried to tell Orpheus. She really had. He had only laughed in her face and said she ought to be flattered, and that he was sure Aristaeus meant no harm. He was a good man, Orpheus insisted. He wouldn't do anything to her. Only once did he begrudgingly go to talk to Aristaeus, but he just came back saying the same things as be- fore, now with more weight to his words because Aristaeus "confirmed" that he was harmless. Afterward he only ever brushed her off when she tried to bring it up again.

She would sometimes ask Orpheus to accompany her on her walks to and from their home, but he would refuse, asking why he should inconvenience himself over her irrational paranoia. There was no danger, he insisted, so she didn't need him. She asked the other nymphs instead, which they readily agreed to. Aristaeus made them all uncomfortable as well, and they knew who his target was. Orpheus still thought they were being silly, but he never said it through more than a roll of his eyes every now and then.

Eurydice stopped going out alone everywhere save for just outside of her own home, but she was to find that she was not safe even there. One day while Orpheus had been away for one of his performances, she'd gone out to her garden to enjoy the sun. She never thought that Aristaeus would approach her at home, but there he was, appearing right beside her with that smile on his face. He proclaimed his feelings for her again, and again she rejected him. This time, however, he did not go kindly.

Aristaeus grabbed her upper arms before she could turn to leave, so hard that she could feel bruises forming under his fingers, and despite her struggling, he...

He didn't violate her, but he'd come dangerously close to it before she managed to escape with those blue marks on her arms. She ran, going wherever took her far away from him. To Orpheus, to other nymphs... whichever she found first. Aristaeus was right behind her, but she was faster, just a little. She would have outrun him, if it weren't for the snake.

She didn't see it, but she felt it when she stepped on it. It was much faster than Aristaeus. It whipped around with a furious hiss and latched onto her ankle. She stumbled from the sudden pain, fell to the ground, and when she understood what was happening, she was already dead.

Death had been a blessing, as it turned out. In Elysium, she'd been able to truly relax for the first time in over a year. She could be alone without worrying about being watched by someone, she didn't have to ask someone to escort her anywhere, and no one touched her if she didn't want them to. She could just be and be happy.

Eurydice hugged herself tight. No. She did not think she could return to a life of fear again, always looking over her shoulder, barely leaving her home for fear that Aristaeus would be waiting. That was no way to live. Much as she loved Orpheus, she couldn't do it. He wouldn't do anything to help her, either. He'd proven that much. He barely even tried to believe her—what would happen if Aristaeus grabbed her again and this time she couldn't escape? What would Orpheus do, what would he say? Who would he blame?

He would blame who all the other men blamed. She'd seen it happen before. It was best he let her go now while she still loved him, because she knew that if he forced her right back to where she'd left off, she would surely hate him before the year was up.

They were almost to the exit. She could see the sky again, and the grass and flowers and trees. She could hear the birds singing their sweet songs, and she could feel the breeze tickle her skin. The sun returned the beautiful bronze color to Orpheus' skin and revealed the specks of gold in his curly hair. She reached out to touch him, but her hand passed right through his back. He didn't seem to notice.

Eurydice took a breath. "Orpheus," she said, and by the way his steps faltered for a moment she knew he'd heard her. "I ...I want to see you. Look at me. Please."

He hesitated, then replied, "I can't. You'll be taken from me again."

"We're almost there, and I can't hardly stand it any longer. Just a quick glance won't hurt. Trust me?"

His pace slowed, and after a moment, just before reaching the top of the tunnel, he very slowly turned his head. She saw his cheek, his nose, his lips, and one bright blue eye.

Then he turned fully toward her, face contorted in despair as she was pulled back, back, back down the tunnel with a smile on her face.

2020 Awards

Editor's Choice Award
Chosen by the Editor-in-Chief
Prose: "The Underground Hotel" by Jordan Beamer
Poetry: "Pembroke Retirement Home" by Andrew Cooper-Stone

English Faculty Award
Sponsored by the English Faculty of CNU
Prose: "Flanders' Mud" by Raleigh Hampson
Poetry: "Anamnesis" by Regan Flieg

Currents is funded through the generous donations of individuals and companies. Their donations not only allow us to publish the journal, but create educational opportunities in writing, editing, publishing, management, and literary production. If you would like to be a Currents supporter, please see our website for information or contact us at currents@cnu.edu

Thanks to our 2020 donors for making this journal possible.

Financial support provided by:
Dr. Ivan Rodden
Rachel Applebach

In kind support provided by:
Department of English, Christopher Newport University
College of Arts and Humanities, Christopher Newport University
Trible Library, Christopher Newport University

9 798718 276572